Trapped!

To Aila,

Happy Birthday!
:)

Best Wishes,

Michele Montz Bow
(Michele)

Trapped!

Michele Martin Bossley

James Lorimer & Company Ltd., Publishers
Toronto, 2002

James Lorimer & Company Ltd. acknowledges the support of the
Ontario Arts Council. We acknowledge the support of the
Government of Canada through the Book Publishing Industry
Development Program (BPIDP) for our publishing activities. We
acknowledge the support of the Canada Council for the Arts for our
publishing program.

Cover illustration: Greg Ruhl

Canada Cataloguing in Publication Data

Bossley, Michele Martin
    Trapped!

(Sports stories ; 53)
ISBN 1-55028-759-1 (bound).—ISBN 1-55028-758-3 (pbk.)

I. Title. II. Series: Sports stories (Toronto, Ont.) ; 53.

PS8553.O7394T73 2002   jC813'.54   C2002-900199-4
PZ7.B64952Tr 2002

James Lorimer & Company Ltd.,   Distributed in the United States by:
Publishers   Orca Book Publishers,
35 Britain Street   P.O. Box 468
Toronto, Ontario   Custer, WA USA
M5A 1R7   98240-0468
www.lorimer.ca

Printed and bound in Canada.

Contents

Acknowledgements

The thank-you's for this book are many and heartfelt — to Jessica Robertshaw for answering innumerable questions about U-14 soccer, for letting me sit in on her games, and for reading this manuscript for accuracy, to her parents Sandra and Jim for their help, to Brent Morrison and my husband Mike for sharing their knowledge of soccer, to Pamela Perizzolo for answering questions about grade eight Foods, to Scot Urquhart for saving me from a computer-virus disaster while on deadline, and finally, to Katie Young, whose own real-life adventures with teacher troubles inspired Jane's story.

1

Tryouts

My red pinney had come untied and flapped uncomfortably over one shoulder. I grabbed it as I ran and shoved it down, my eyes never leaving the ball. A swirl of black and white, it shot down the field into our defensive zone. The forwards from both teams thundered after it, but I ducked sideways, realizing that adding to the cluster of players was not a good idea.

"Hey, Reds!" I yelled. "Let the defence handle it! Get back in position!" My team either didn't hear or ignored me. I headed for an open patch, where I could accept a pass if one of my teammates got the ball.

Another girl on my team, red-faced and sweaty, was fighting for control. She spotted me to the side, and took the ball away from the knot of bodies with a kick aimed toward the sky.

"Forwards! Heads up!" she hollered.

I saw the ball coming. I danced beneath it, gauging where it would fall. Should I trap it? Head it?

It was coming straight down — not a great chance to head it out without scrambling my brains in the process. I used my thighs to stop it, then snagged it with my foot and started sprinting for the goal. There was no one to pass to — all my mid-fielders and the other forwards hadn't caught up yet, and their defence was coming up on me hard. I ran, my breath catching in my side, dodging the yellow-pinney players, my eyes on the goal.

"Jane, pass back!"

I heard the cry, but I was almost there. Panting, I aimed for the upper corner when a yellow player suddenly vaulted side-ways, digging for the ball. I was going too fast to dodge, and I went down with the other player in a tangle of feet and legs, the ball shooting out from under us. The grass was damp and slick under my legs, and I slid on my stomach before coming to a stop. Karianne, the yellow player who had tripped me, landed hard on her side. We both stared at each other before trying stiffly to get up. The smell of wet earth filled my nose, and my entire front was streaked with mud.

"You okay?" I asked.

"Sort of." Karianne brushed herself off, examining a long red mark on her thigh from skidding on the grass.

The coaches had stopped play, motioning everyone in from the field.

Karianne and I trotted over to the sidelines, where the coaches were collecting the pinneys. I pulled mine off and wait-ed as one of the coaches approached.

"Jane, that was some spectacular running out there," he said.

I started to smile.

"But your passing was a no-show. You've got to think strat-egy out there, okay? I realize that the mid-field went too far into the defensive zone, and you were alone, but there are ways to stall for time until you have backup, or you could have passed back and moved into a scoring position. Instead, you lost the ball. You have to think teamwork."

My smile faded.

He turned to Karianne. "And Karianne, we like to see play-ers who aren't afraid to be aggressive, but tripping a player will get you carded."

"But I didn't mean to!" Karianne protested.

"A ref might not see it that way." The coach took Karianne's yellow pinney. "Third tryout is on Wednesday. See you then." He walked away, leaving Karianne and me looking at the ground.

"Great," Karianne muttered. "Nice way to end the tryout."

"It'll be okay," I said.

"No, it won't!" Karianne whirled around, looking suddenly ferocious. "Don't you see, Jane? To make Division One, you have be perfect in tryouts. There are so many girls who want to play on this team, it's unbelievable. You and I are on our way back to Division Two. It's over." She stomped away.

I watched her go, standing there until I was the last one on the field. I rubbed my temple and took a deep breath. I would like to play Division One — who wouldn't? Division One was made up of the best players in the whole city. But I liked just being here, being a part of soccer.

A forgotten ball was wedged under the branches of a pine tree near the fence, and I walked over and pulled it out. I looked quickly, but the coaches were gone. I'd have to give the ball back next time.

I gave in to the impulse of running on the deserted field, and dealt the ball a mighty kick. It spun wildly in the air, and I ran after it. The grass was still brown, but sprouts of green were showing through, and I could hear it swishing against my cleats. The sky was grey with drizzly rain waiting to fall. The wind was cold and clear, making my legs itch as the blood pounded through them. The air carried a fresh smell from somewhere that could only be spring. I ran, dribbling the ball, faking passes to imaginary teammates, before I took a shot on the empty net. It sailed through the upper corner, and I grinned to myself.

This was soccer, no matter what team I was on.

2

A New Friend

Rats." I stared at the crumpled sheets of homework. Ms. Horvath had handed the written assignment back just before the bell and the red-penned grade was circled several times. And not because it was good.

Sighing, I dug into my lunch bag. Ms. Horvath really knew how to wreck a perfectly good meal. I'd been starved when I sat down in the lunchroom, but not anymore.

"Jane?"

I looked up. Ashley Petrie stood there.

"Um, do you mind if I sit with you? It's pretty crowded today."

"Sure." I gestured toward the empty chair.

Ashley dragged the chair out and sat down, her feet making a squelching noise when she moved.

"What's with the shoes?" I asked, unwrapping my sandwich.

"Someone spilled root beer by the door. Guess who stepped in it?" Ashley looked a little embarrassed. "I'm such a geek. I'm sticking to the floor every time I move."

I smiled at her. "You're not a geek." I didn't know Ashley very well, but she seemed nice. She wasn't in any of my classes, and she'd just started at my school last fall. "Just unlucky."

"An unlucky geek, then." But she smiled back.

I took another bite of sandwich, and pulled an orange and a few cookies out of my bag.

Ashley's smile became fixed. "What are you eating?" She

tried not to look horrified.

I glanced down at my lunch. "A sandwich, an orange and chocolate chip cookies."

"But … the bread is *green!*" Ashley stared at it.

I grinned. "It's not mould or anything. It's made with ground spinach. That's why it's green."

"Oh." Ashley swallowed. "Your mom makes some … uh … interesting stuff."

"Oh, my mom didn't make this. I did."

"*You did?*"

"Sure. The bread is terrific. My brothers practically inhaled the whole thing, but I managed to save some for my lunch. Want to try?" I held up the sandwich.

Ashley looked hesitant, but she leaned forward and took a small bite. "Hey," she said, chewing. "This is amazing! You can't even taste the spinach."

"I know," I said proudly. "My mom makes my brothers and me eat spinach for dinner because she says it's so healthy, but we all hate it. So, I decided to try something else with it and get her off our backs. Bread is actually pretty easy to make. I love doing it, because it smells so good when it's baking."

"Wow. You must be an awesome cook."

"I wish. I'm, like, flunking Foods. Ms. Horvath thinks I'm a bozo. I just have fun fooling around in the kitchen. My brothers will eat almost anything and they're always starved, so practically everything I make gets eaten."

"Have you ever made anything really gross?"

"Oh, yeah!" I started laughing. "One of the worst was the chocolate yogurt milkshakes. They were *disgusting*. But we were out of ice cream so I used plain yogurt with cocoa powder instead. Even my stepbrother wouldn't drink one."

Ashley grinned. "That bad, eh?"

"Let's just say that chocolate isn't supposed to taste sour." I popped the last bite of sandwich into my mouth, just as an older girl walked up and dropped an old, stinky pair of soccer cleats on the table beside Ashley. The girl had brown hair that was streaked with green and held in tufts all over her head by plastic butterfly clips. Silver glitter gleamed on each eyelid, and a gold stud glinted on the right side of her nose. She frowned, first at Ashley, then at me. Startled, I stopped mid-chew, about to tell this girl exactly what she could do with her smelly soccer cleats, but she spoke first.

"You forgot your shoes," she said flatly.

"Oh, uh ... thanks, Tee." Ashley flushed red as the whole table turned to look.

"Yeah, well, I'm not your babysitter, Ash, so remember your stuff, okay?" Tee delivered this speech in a tough voice, but Ashley didn't seem to notice.

"Okay."

"See ya." The girl walked away. Ashley seemed to shrink in her seat.

"Who was that?" I asked.

"My sister, Teagan. She's in grade nine."

I watched her walk out of the lunchroom. Teagan had on low-riding jeans that flared at the ankle and a pink stretch top that was very tight. I would never have guessed they were sisters. Ashley was tall and had soft blonde hair falling out of a ponytail in wisps. She wore an ordinary grey jersey and jeans so well-worn they looked as soft as velvet.

"She seems ... uh ... nice." I crumpled my empty lunch bag and pitched it into a nearby garbage bin.

"She's a jerk," Ashley said flatly.

"A nice jerk," I corrected. We looked at each other and laughed again. I suddenly really liked Ashley. I pointed to the grubby soccer cleats still on the table. "You going out for soccer?"

"Yeah. The last scrimmage tryout is tonight." Ashley dropped the cleats on the floor.

"I know. I'm going, too."

Ashley eyed me. "I didn't see you at the last one. What time did you go?"

"Uh ... eight-thirty."

"That was the Division One tryout." Ashley looked impressed.

"I know. I don't think I'll make Div One, though. There are so many girls who were just awesome — I couldn't believe it. I played Two A last year, but I had a great season, and I guess the coaches wanted to see how I measured up against the next division."

"Wow." Ashley looked envious. "I played Two B, but I really wanted to make A this year."

"You want to go kick the ball around before the bell?"

"Sure!" Ashley picked up her unfinished sandwich and started for the door. "Let's get out there," she said, munching. "I need all the practice I can get."

I stopped and reached under the table, pulling out Ashley's battered cleats. "Then don't forget these!"

3

Soccer Season

"Okay, ladies!" The coach called from across the field. "Come on in!"

I'd been working on passing drills with Sarah, while Ashley was in goal. It was our second practice, and the coaches had us rotating through different positions to see where they wanted to place us.

Karianne had been right. I don't know how good my chances of making Division One were before that tryout, but they definitely weren't great afterwards. Karianne, Sarah, a few other girls who played Division Two last year, and I were bumped back down. There were just too many strong players for us all to make it. I didn't mind that much — it was kind of an honour just to be asked to try out for Division One. But Karianne was pretty ticked off.

"All right." Emily Brunner's dad consulted his clipboard. He was our coach this year — I'd played for him last year and I liked him. He'd been coaching since Emily started playing. I don't know how much soccer Emily's dad played — but I got the feeling it was a lot. Plus he knew the manual inside-out and had been to practically every coaching clinic Calgary offered.

Emily's dad cleared his throat. "I've decided on position assignments for the Hurricanes based on your tryouts and the last few practices. I know some of you might be used to playing a certain position, but I've noticed quite a few of you have skills we can use in other areas of the field. So be prepared here — I'm about to shake things up."

Karianne, who was standing beside me, shifted uneasily.

I raised my hand. "Mr. Jim?"

Emily's dad smiled in my direction. All last year I called him that, because even though he asked the team to call him Jim, most of the girls still called him Mr. Brunner. He said that made him feel like a teacher, so Mr. Jim seemed like a good solution.

"Yes, Jane?" he said.

"Will these positions be permanent? I mean, will we be allowed to switch around at all?"

"These will be your permanent positions, yes. But flexibility is key in soccer, so once we've had a chance to train in these positions, we'll be working on backups. Forwards and mid-fielders can expect to switch around a lot, based on what's happening in the game. But we'll talk about all that in the next few practices. For now, here's where you'll be playing: in goal, Sarah Jacobsen. Ashley Petrie, sweeper. Defence is Emily Brunner, Karianne Phipps —"

I heard Karianne suck in her breath, and I sneaked a quick glance at her. Her lips were folded into a wobbly line and she was blinking faster than normal. At first I wondered why she was upset — there was nothing wrong with playing defence — and then I remembered that she had played in goal all last year. Mr. Jim wasn't kidding when he said he was going to shake things up!

"Jane? Are you with me, Jane?" Mr. Jim was looking at me.

"Huh? Oh, yeah. I'm with you."

"Good. Because you're the Hurricane's centre forward this year. So I need to make sure you're paying attention."

Centre! Mr. Jim wanted me in centre? That's the position usually reserved for the best scorer on the team. I was a forward last year, but almost never in centre. I couldn't help grinning at this news.

"Okay, team. If there aren't any questions, then I'll see you all at next practice." Mr. Jim stuck his pen back in his clipboard, and everyone else started to gather up jackets and gym bags. Everyone except Karianne.

"Um, Coach Brunner?" She stepped forward. Her voice sounded so high-pitched and urgent, I paused to listen.

"Yes, Karianne?"

"I was wondering why you didn't put me in as keeper. I've played goal for the last three years."

"I know, Karianne." Mr. Jim's voice was kind. "And you're good in goal. But I think you have skills we can use out in the field, and I'd like to try some new talent in goal this year."

"In other words, you think Sarah is better than me," Karianne said bitterly.

"Not better, necessarily. But she has some good skills, and I'd like to give her a chance. Give defence a try, Karianne. You might really like it."

Karianne turned away, but I heard her muttering under her breath. "Yeah, right. The way I like liver for breakfast." She picked her bag up in a hurry and stomped off.

I gathered my things. I saw Ashley waiting for me partway down the field, and hurried to catch up.

"Congrats on being striker!" She gave me a high-five.

"Thanks!"

"Karianne didn't look too happy." Ashley didn't know many of the players on our team — only five members of our Hurricanes team went to the same school — but she knew Karianne from gym class.

"Playing goal is practically Karianne's life," I said. "I don't know why, really. She's not that good. I think she's better on the field than in goal."

"I thought she was asked to try out for Division One this year."

"She was, but I can't figure that out. Her team made the Division Two city championships last year, then lost the final game. Maybe that's why — they picked people from the top two Div Two teams to try out for Div One."

"You weren't on Karianne's team?"

"No. We made semi-finals, then dumped it. I won MVP for the season, though. Maybe that's why they bumped me up in the tryouts." I shifted my soccer bag to the other shoulder. "What about you? Where did you play last year?"

Ashley looked uncomfortable. "Uh … with Northside. We moved to this neighbourhood last August."

"What did you play?"

"Sweeper, mostly. Sometimes I was in goal."

I eyed her. "You don't seem bossy enough for sweeper. Or goalie."

Ashley turned red. "I'm not … you know … into yelling or whatever. But I like the strategy. I like organizing the plays. I think of it more as coaching than being bossy."

"Karianne thinks of it as being bossy," I said. We both giggled.

4

Cooking Chaos

Boys and girls!" Ms. Horvath clapped her hands sharply. "Settle down, please!"

I frowned. Ms. Horvath always made Foods such a drag. With a lot of chair-scraping and shuffling around, the class settled into their seats. I was already at my table with Nicholas Garvey and Karianne, who were in my group.

"Today, we will continue our module on baking basics. By now you should have completed the homework on the six different types of cookies, and you can apply that knowledge to the rolled cookies we'll be working on in this class. Each group will use its assigned recipe, which I have left at each cooking station. You may now get started."

Nicholas, Karianne and I stood up and moved toward our kitchen area, which was closest to the door.

Nicholas grabbed the recipe off the counter. "Ooh, yum, Karianne. We're making booger cookies today." He flashed her a heart-stopping grin.

"Give me that, you weirdo!" Karianne snatched the paper away. I don't think she cared that Nicholas was one of the best-looking guys in grade eight, even though lots of girls did. "We're making ginger cookies, Nicholas. Ginger. Not booger." She pointed to the top of the recipe.

"Whoops. My mistake." Nicholas grinned at me this time.

There was a sharp knock on the open door. I glanced up.

Ashley's sister Teagan was standing there. Today her hair stood up in stiff spikes and she had a fake tattoo of a rose on the side of her neck. At least, I think it was fake.

Ms. Horvath came to the door. "What is it, Teagan? I'm in the middle of a class."

"The principal said I had to come and talk to you about making up the classes I missed." Teagan seemed uncomfortable with everyone watching her.

"Why don't you come in at lunch hour," suggested Ms. Horvath. "I'll have more time to talk to you then."

"Okay." Teagan turned on her heel and walked out.

"Back to work, everyone," Ms. Horvath said. "Your batter must be mixed and rolled out soon, because the cookies have to be in the oven by a quarter to eleven or they won't have enough time to bake before the bell."

"She is so strange," Karianne said.

"Ms. Horvath?" I asked.

"No." Karianne shot me a withering stare. "That girl. Teagan-whoever."

"Ashley's sister?" I said without thinking.

"That's Ashley Petrie's sister?" Karianne's eyes widened.

"Yeah. So?" I was sorry I'd said anything. But it wasn't a secret. I figured Karianne already knew that.

"Nothing. I've just heard stuff about her, that's all."

"What kind of stuff?"

"Never mind. Let's get back to work." Karianne fell to reading the recipe intently. "Jane, can you get out two eggs and separate the yolks from the whites? We need the whites to glaze the cookies after we get them cut out. Bozo and I will start mixing up the batter." She gave Nicholas a nudge with her elbow.

I just nodded and reached for the small mixing bowl, then turned to the fridge. I took out a couple of eggs and laid them on the counter while I reached for a spoon.

"Nicholas!" Karianne screeched. "Watch what you're doing!"

I looked up to see Nicholas holding the electric mixer out of the bowl. The beaters were still whirling, and he was trying to find the stop button. Splats of butter were everywhere, including down the front of Karianne.

Nicholas finally found the button and shut off the mixer. "Sorry, Karianne."

"Sorry!" Karianne snorted. She tried to brush the clods of butter off her sweater, but only succeeded in smearing them in. "Look at me!"

I tried not to giggle. Karianne did look pretty funny. But then I heard a soft crunch behind me, followed by a second. I turned to see my eggs, broken on the floor. They'd rolled off the edge of the counter.

Of course, Ms. Horvath chose that moment to check on us. "What is going on here?"

Karianne gave her sweater another swipe with a damp dish-cloth. "Nicholas couldn't figure out how to turn the mixer off."

"I see." She frowned slightly. "Nicholas, it's always a good idea to keep the mixer in the bowl until you shut it off. Karianne, this is why we have aprons for you to wear. I suggest you find yours. And Jane, what is this on the floor?"

It seemed obvious to me. "Two eggs."

"Why are they there?"

"They rolled off the counter."

"I have told you in class before this to remove the entire carton of eggs from the refrigerator and then use the eggs you need, to avoid this very problem. Weren't you listening?"

Probably not. "Yes."

"Then why didn't you do it?"

"I forgot."

"That's not acceptable."

Seems like nothing I do in this class is, I thought. "I'm sorry."

Ms. Horvath sighed. "Jane, let's not have a repeat of last term. Please remember in the future."

"I will," I promised, feeling the heat rise in my cheeks as I remembered my first term in CTS. CTS stood for Career and Technology Studies, and Ms. Horvath taught most of the classes. Foods, Fashions, all that stuff. We had done sewing, and it had been a disaster. I was always getting in trouble, but the worst was when I tried to make pants, and ended up sewing them to the sleeve of my sweatshirt. It had taken Ms. Horvath and the janitor almost an hour to free me from the sewing machine.

She moved on to the next group, and I exhaled in relief. Nicholas and Karianne began to add sugar to the butter. I reached into the fridge and pulled out the carton of eggs.

I cracked two eggs into the bowl and tossed the shells in the garbage. I stared at them for a few minutes, thinking. Then I looked up. "Karianne?"

"Uh?" Karianne was packing brown sugar into a little scoop.

"How do you separate eggs?"

"How should I know? Nicholas, how many scoops have we added?"

"You're asking me?" Nicholas was using the electric mixer again.

"Augh!" Karianne groaned.

I turned back to my eggs. Well, the most obvious thing to use was a spoon. I picked up the spoon I'd grabbed earlier for the glaze. It looked like it was about the right size. I slid it underneath one of the egg yolks and gently tried to lift it out of the white. It jiggled and slithered, then slid right off the spoon back into the bowl.

"Darn." I tried again, this time lifting it more quickly, but the whole thing just fell right off the spoon and splatted back into the bowl. There had to be an easier way to do this. I slid the spoon underneath one more time, but this time I noticed that blobs of yellow had escaped into the white part. The yolk had broken.

"Rats!" I muttered. I got a second bowl and started trying to fish out each little blob of yellow, but every time I tried to get the spoon under one, it seemed to escape and split into more, smaller blobs.

"Jane, *what* are you doing?"

I looked up to see Ms. Horvath behind me. "Separating eggs," I said.

"With a spoon?" Ms. Horvath glared at me.

"Well, yes. What else am I supposed to use?"

"This." Ms. Horvath strode to the supply drawer in our station and removed a little cup-like thingy with slits on the side. "This is an egg separator, Jane. You would know this if you had been paying attention during the utensils section of the unit. You would also know this if you had completed the homework for that section."

I bristled inside. I *had* done the homework, but was I supposed to remember absolutely everything in this course?

"I don't think even the best chefs in the world could separate an egg with a teaspoon," Ms. Horvath said, examining my eggs.

"It won't matter, will it? I can pick out most of the yolk," I said.

"It will matter. Egg whites can't be used if even a little bit of yolk is in them. Meringues won't fluff up, angel cakes won't rise, and glaze won't harden properly if the yolk is mixed in with the white." Ms. Horvath tipped the bowl and swirled the eggs. "Jane, you have just managed to waste four eggs in the five minutes you have been cooking. I can't afford to keep you in my class at this rate."

"I'm sorry."

"Why don't you help Karianne mix the batter. Nicholas can take over the glaze."

"Okay."

Ms. Horvath turned to Karianne. "Have you two already added the egg to your batter?"

"Yes." Karianne had been watching me get into trouble.

Ms. Horvath sighed. "We could have used Jane's eggs if you hadn't." She reached for some plastic wrap, tore a piece off and wrapped up the bowl. "Put these in the refrigerator please, Jane. Maybe I can find something to do with them."

I took the bowl quickly and turned toward the fridge, bumping into Nicholas in the process. I heard Ms. Horvath suck in her breath.

I deposited the eggs safely into the refrigerator, and Ms. Horvath moved on to the next group.

"I hate this class," I muttered.

"Same here," Karianne said. She handed me the recipe. "Tell me how much flour."

I scanned the list of ingredients. "Twelve cups."

"Twelve cups? Are you sure?"

"That's what it says." I looked at the recipe. The numbers were spaced a little bit apart, but that's what they said: twelve. "See?"

Karianne squinted at the paper. "I forgot my contacts."

"Well, it says twelve. So hurry up. I can't wait to get out of here."

"Okay." Karianne began scooping the flour. "You stir." She took a butter knife and carefully smoothed it across the top of the scoop.

"What are you doing?" I asked.

"We're supposed to do it this way, to make sure we have exactly the right measurement."

"Oh, for Pete's sake!" I said, exasperated. "We'll be here all day if you do it like that. I bake stuff at home all the time, and I just scoop the flour and dump it in."

"Ms. Horvath said to do it like this." Karianne started on the second scoop. I rolled my eyes, but kept my mouth shut and stirred the dough as Karianne measured each cup with painstaking care. At around the eight-cup point, I could hardly stir it anymore.

"It's like concrete," I said.

Karianne looked dismayed. "I don't think this is how it's supposed to be."

I had a bad feeling she was right, and I just didn't need any more headaches with Ms. Horvath today. Before I could say anything, though, Karianne's hand had shot into the air.

"Ms. Horvath?" Karianne called. "I think we did something wrong."

Ms. Horvath closed her eyes briefly, like she was praying or something. Then she strode over. "What's the matter?"

"The batter seems a little … thick," I said, letting go of the wooden spoon.

Ms. Horvath surveyed the mess in the bowl. "You've added too much flour."

Karianne turned on me. "I told you so!"

"How much did you add?" Ms. Horvath asked.

"Uh … about seven cups or so," I said.

"More like eight," Karianne amended.

"Eight! Why on earth would you put in that much?"

"Jane told me to." Karianne said quickly.

I glared at her.

"Jane?" Ms. Horvath waited for an explanation.

"The recipe says twelve cups!" I protested. "Look!"

Ms. Horvath took the sheet of paper and read it. She closed her eyes again. "Give me strength," she muttered. "Jane, there's a problem with the photocopying here. It's supposed to read one and a half cups, but the second one and the slash aren't really visible. I can see why you might think it's a twelve, but good heavens, can you really believe that a cookie recipe that has other ingredients in much smaller quantities would call for *that* much flour?"

"I told her I thought it was wrong," Karianne put in.

"Karianne, you're not helping," I whispered through clenched teeth.

"Jane, you should have asked me." Ms. Horvath looked sadly at the bowl. "The eggs were bad enough, but these cookies are ruined."

"I didn't want to get in any more trouble," I said.

"Well, that's a theory that didn't quite work, did it?" Ms. Horvath shook her head at me. "I'm sorry, Jane, but I have no choice but to give your group a failing grade for this assignment."

"What?" Karianne looked startled. "Ms. Horvath, that's not fair. Nicholas and I were doing it right!"

Ms. Horvath paused. "You and Nicholas can stay behind. We'll discuss the possibility of a make-up assignment. Jane, you can dump this mess and the three of you can get started cleaning up." She walked away.

"Thanks a lot, Jane!" Karianne hissed as I pulled the cover off the garbage can.

"Same to you!" I retorted. "You read the recipe, too — why did you blame it all on me?"

"I told you, I forgot my contacts. I couldn't read the numbers that well. Besides, you were the one who told me to hurry up and just do it."

I shook my head. The argument was pointless. Nicholas was wisely staying silent, running the hot water into the sink to start washing up. Ms. Horvath thought I was an idiot. My grade in this class had just sunk to an all-time low. There wasn't much more to say.

5

Finders Keepers

Jane, have you seen my wallet? It was in here with my soccer stuff, and now I can't find it." Sarah was pawing through her sports bag.

"It's probably in this mess somewhere." I looked at the tangle of jackets, mitts and boots piled at the edge of the field. A spring snowstorm had hit Calgary last night, and it had been cold enough this morning that everyone dug out their winter gear again. But the sun had been warm today, and the fields were dry enough to play. I was wearing a fleece top under my team shirt, though. The wind was freezing.

Sarah gave me a wry grin. "I hope so. My birthday money from my grandma is in it. I'd hate to lose it."

"What are you going to buy?" I asked.

"A soccer ball."

"A soccer ball? Don't you have one already?"

"We have two, actually. But my sisters always hog them. Besides, I want my *own*."

I nodded in understanding. With three brothers in the house, I knew what it felt like to never have something that was just mine. The only things I can honestly say I never have to share are my toothbrush and my underwear. And I'm sure if I wore boys' jockeys, I'd have to share those, too.

Mr. Jim gestured impatiently from farther down the field. "Sarah, Jane, let's go get warmed up."

Sarah abandoned the search. "I'll have to find it later." We ran out to join the others in some easy laps around our half of the field. Then Mr. Jim had us stretch out, especially our legs. He said we could easily tear muscles or tendons in soccer, because of the bursts of speed players have to use during the game.

I did some passing drills with Ashley. Running up and back, we practised trapping the ball and controlling it without watching our feet.

Finally Mr. Jim blew the whistle, and we ran back in, panting. "Nice handling," I said to Ashley.

"Thanks." She reached for her water bottle. I saw Teagan sitting on the grass, and waved. She frowned, then gave a half-hearted wave back.

"Teagan's here," I said to Ashley.

"I know. My dad's picking us up after the game. She's not too thrilled about waiting around."

Before I could comment, Mr. Jim motioned for us to move in. "All right, girls. Our Hurricanes team is a strong one this year. Some of you played for me last year, some of you played for different teams, and some of you are new to the division. I can tell you that my team placed third in the divisional championships last year, and I think that this year's team is talented enough to go all the way. But to do that, we have to make every game count. I need every one of you to give me your all, every second that you're on the field. Are you with me?"

"Yeah!" we shouted.

"Okay! Take a minute to get your equipment on, if you haven't already, and get a drink of water. The game starts in five minutes."

Sarah reached for her sports bag. The zipper was open, and she rummaged inside. Then she stopped and peered into the interior.

"What's the matter?" I asked, between sips of water.

"My cleats are missing. They were brand-new! I was going to put them on before warm-ups, but I didn't have time, and now they're gone!"

"Are you sure?" I knelt down to look.

"Yes. My wallet was in there, too. Someone took my stuff!"

"Mr. Jim," I called. "We have a problem here."

"What's going on?" Mr. Jim came over.

"My stuff is missing. Both my wallet and my cleats."

"It's probably here somewhere. Who could tell in this mess?" Mr. Jim eyed the piles of jackets and bags.

"It's not. I looked."

"Do you have your old cleats?" Mr. Jim asked.

Sarah shook her head. "No, they're too small. I left them at home."

"You'll have to play in your running shoes, Sarah," Mr. Jim said.

Sarah swiped the grass with the toe of her sneaker. "The grass is really slippery from the snow last night. It'll be harder to dig in to jump and dive."

"Maybe I'd better put in a backup. I hate to pull you, Sarah, but I don't want you getting injured because you're sliding around out there."

"I can handle it," Sarah said quickly, but Mr. Jim shook his head.

"What's going on?" The rest of the team gathered around.

"I have to pull Sarah from goal," Mr. Jim answered. "Ashley, you're in."

Everyone looked stunned. "Not Karianne?" Ashley squeaked. Karianne stared straight ahead, her face like a stone.

"No. You have a goalie jersey?"

Ashley shook her head.

"You'll have to borrow Sarah's. Sarah, you go in as sweeper."

"Why isn't Sarah playing goal?" Emily asked.

Mr. Jim looked stern. "Her cleats are missing. Apparently, so is her wallet."

Ashley's face registered shock. "Who would do that?"

I shrugged. "No idea. But the cleats are brand-new, and she

had birthday money in the wallet."

"Birthday money?" Ashley's voice went a notch higher. "How much?"

I looked at Sarah.

"Thirty dollars," she said defiantly.

"Where was your bag?" Ashley asked.

"Near the end, by the bench. Why?" Sarah asked.

"No reason," Ashley muttered.

"Hopefully it's just buried under all this mess." Mr. Jim frowned at the piles of bags, jackets and assorted bags of chips and Slurpee cups. "Let's try and keep better track of our stuff, gang. This is a soccer field, not the city dump."

Sarah looked furious. She tied her running shoes into double knots, snapping the laces so tightly I was sure she'd never get them undone again. "My stuff was in my bag," she grumbled. "I didn't leave it lying around."

"I know." I stayed beside her. "Try not to worry about it now, Sarah. We have a game."

"I know that!" Sarah stood up.

"Let's get out there, girls!" Mr. Jim gestured to us to get on the field.

I lined up for the kick-off. We were playing against the Westglen Wildcats, and I knew from experience that they were usually pretty good.

I hoped Sarah could keep her mind on the game. The ref blew the whistle. I wrested the ball away from the opposing centre, dribbling it sideways and sending a pass to Jen, who was playing left forward. The other team intercepted it and sped down the field, controlling the ball with some great passing. I doubled back to help the mid-fielders, but the Wildcats broke through our defence and I saw Ashley tense up, waiting for the shot. The Wildcats forward sent a powerful kick toward our goal, but Karianne ran for it just outside the goalie box, trying to intercept the ball. It bounced upward from the side of her foot, and ricocheted off her arm.

The ref blew the whistle. "Hand ball. Penalty kick, Wild-cats." He placed the ball to the side of the goal, outside the box, and motioned for a Hurricane player to take her position.

"All right girls, don't let them get it in there. Make a wall, make it tight!" I heard Mr. Jim hollering.

All of our mid-fielders crammed against each other, trying to make a solid wall of bodies that the ball could not penetrate, while the defence tried to keep the other team covered. I wished I could get in there, too. I felt like I was just standing around doing nothing, but my team needed me to be available to pick up a pass, should they be able to work the ball down the field.

The Wildcats forward was clever. She looked like she was just going to belt that ball straight at our players, who were cringing with arms wrapped protectively across their chests, with one fist in front of each of their faces. But instead, the forward changed momentum and dealt the ball a gentle side pass to another forward who was positioned near the middle of the goalie box. That forward was quick and fired the shot at Ashley before anyone had time to react. I thought it was a goal for sure.

But Ashley was lightning quick — she slammed her body down hard and caught the ball in her midsection, wrapping her arms around it so it wouldn't escape. Then she stood up tri-umphantly and gave the ball a deft kick, sending it far down the field — toward me. I sprinted toward it, and corralled it between my feet, keeping an eye on the defensive players who had remained near their zone for just such a reason. I had no one to pass to. My forwards were behind me, and I was facing these players alone. Then I remembered my mistake at tryouts, and cast a glance over my shoulder. Jen was pounding up behind me.

"Jen!" I yelled, then slipped the ball backwards for her to take. She dribbled it neatly, giving me a chance to work into the defence without moving past them, which would get us called for offside. Then, just before a Wildcats player could reach her to try and steal the ball, she sent the ball to me. I turned and blasted a shot at the goal. The keeper gloved it out, sending the ball skittering back onto the field, but I snagged it and took a second shot. This time the goalie wasn't so quick, and the ball flew through the goal posts and buried itself in the net.

"Way to go, Jane!" I heard Ashley yell from down field.

Mr. Jim signalled for us to switch off. I ran for the bench and gulped down some water.

"Great aggressive play out there, Jane. Nice way to keep after it!" Mr. Jim beamed at me before turning to watch the action on the field.

Karianne scowled, then stared sullenly out at the field, taking an occasional swig of water. She gave me a nasty look. "What's your problem?" she snapped, when she caught me looking at her.

"Nothing," I said. Emily, who was sitting on the bench beside me, raised her eyebrows. I responded with a shrug. I had no idea what was bothering Karianne. We were playing well, and we were ahead 1–0. Karianne should have been as excited as the rest of us, but she was like a porcupine with a headache for the rest of the game — prickly and miserable and generally someone to avoid. But nobody else really noticed.

We won 2–0. Ashley had seven shots taken on her, and she didn't let a single one in.

Mr. Jim was very impressed. "Maybe I'll have to talk Sarah into letting me play you in goal for half games," he said, clapping her on the shoulder when she came in from the field.

"You were totally awesome," I told her.

Ashley shrugged off the praise. "Luck," she said.

"Skill," I countered.

"Baloney," Karianne muttered under her breath, just loud enough for Ashley to hear. She picked up her bag and walked away.

6

Chef Jane

Hey, Janey! Slap some more of those eggs on here." Trent leaned back in his seat and held out his plate.

I took the fry pan off the stove and scooped another spoonful onto his plate. When I woke up at six a.m., I felt so good about winning the game that I kept going over it in my head and I couldn't fall back to sleep. So finally, I got up and made breakfast for everybody, something I don't usually do on a Monday.

Trent was the first downstairs after me. He was the middle brother, but only by four months. My stepbrother Joey was also fifteen, and Adam was seventeen.

"Hey, what smells so good?" Adam stuck his head into the kitchen on his way to the upstairs shower.

"Janey made breakfast. Better pull up a chair before Joe gets here."

"Wow, what's the occasion?" Adam abandoned his towel and toothbrush on the stairs and sat down at the table.

"Woke up early, couldn't sleep." I spooned out some eggs on a plate and added a few pieces of toast that were keeping warm in the toaster oven. I'd chopped up a few tomatoes and some sandwich ham, grated a pile of cheddar cheese, and added that to the eggs as they cooked.

"This is awesome!" Adam filled his mouth.

"I know." Trent held out his plate again. "Is there more?"

"Yes, but it's for Joey and me and Dad." My mother doesn't

usually eat big breakfasts, so I knew we didn't have to save any for her.

"Aw, come on, Janey."

"No. Joey's going to want some, too." I sat down at the table with my own plate.

"He got the shower first. He doesn't deserve any," Trent argued.

"Deserve any what?" Mom came downstairs, stepping on Adam's toothbrush. "Ow. Who left this here?" She held it up, its bristles sadly squashed.

"Me. Sorry, Mom." Adam retrieved it and stuck it in the pocket of his bathrobe.

"Eeeuuw!" I said. "You're not going to use it, are you?"

Adam shrugged. "Mom's feet are clean."

I shook my head as Joey came downstairs, still toweling his hair. It stuck out in wet brown spikes.

"Breakfast is on the stove," I told him, taking another bite of my eggs. "Trent's trying to eat yours."

"So what else is new?" Joey draped the wet towel across the back of a chair and helped himself.

"Joseph Evans, get that wet towel off that chair this second!" Mom growled. She reached into the cupboard for the coffee filters. "You'll wreck the wood."

Joey dropped the towel on the linoleum and sat down with his full plate. I saw Mom frown at the towel, but she didn't comment.

"You'd better hurry up, Jane, or you'll be late for school," Mom said.

Adam finished shoveling food into his mouth and stood up. "It's okay, Mom. I'll drop Janey off. I finished the tune-up on my car last night."

"So the Dumpster is actually running now?" I asked. Adam bought his car with the money he earned working part-time at the grocery store, and it is truly pathetic. It's a 1987 Plymouth Reliant that has rust spots retouched with the wrong color of blue paint and a taillight that has been permanently taped to the car with layers of silver duct tape. Adam thinks it's fantastic.

"Careful, Squirt. Don't insult my car, or I won't take you any-where, even if you did make a great breakfast." Adam grinned.

I grinned back and Adam dumped his plate in the sink and went upstairs to shower. It was nice of Adam to offer to drive me. It meant that he'd be at school a lot earlier than he needed to — Trent and Joe too, if they wanted to catch a ride — since my school started earlier than the high school.

I finished eating, grabbed my lunch from the fridge and went upstairs. I ran a brush through my hair and sprayed it with a water bottle to make sure there was no bed-head at the back. I usually have a bath at night, just to avoid the traffic jam for the shower around here. Between my brothers and my stepdad, it's almost never free.

I dabbed some anti-zit cream on my chin, which was looking sort of blotchy, and threw on my favorite jeans with the patched bum and a faded red sweatshirt that used to belong to Joey. Then I picked up my homework, shoved it into my backpack and ran back downstairs. Even if I hadn't been in a hurry, I hate to waste time on my hair and makeup. If there's a reason why I want to look nice, I do, but most of the time I just don't care.

Trent was rummaging in the basket for clean clothes as I came through the laundry room to get my blue jacket — the one with the waterproof shell — from the hook by the garage door. "Hey, I'm not ready yet," he said.

"Tough," I said. I pulled on my jacket. "Adam and I have to go."

"How come he's driving *you*? Me and Joe are going to freeze waiting for the bus." Trent yanked out a shirt, which turned out to be mine.

"Because she made me breakfast," Adam showed up, jingling his keys. "Which is more than I can say for you. Come on, Squirt."

"Besides, it's above freezing, Trent," I said.

"How do you know?"

"Because it's raining."

"Oh, that's great. Thanks, Jane. That makes me feel a lot better."

I followed Adam out the back door, into the gusting rain. "Bye, Mom!" I called. Adam has to park in the back alley, since our garage is only big enough to fit two cars, and Mom and Dad refuse to park theirs outside to make room for the Dumpster.

Adam unlocked the door, got behind the wheel and reached over to unlock my side, while slushy rain slid down my neck. A brother's chivalry will only go so far, I guess.

Adam dropped me off in front of the junior high, and I ran for the doors. The teachers had let the kids wait inside in the hall for the bell, and I wriggled through the crowd, looking for Ashley.

I spotted her blond ponytail near the hallway, and moved closer, but stopped when I saw Teagan. They were standing together, arguing about something. Nobody else was paying any attention.

"Get lost, Ash. I'm not doing anything."

"You're lying!" I'd never heard Ashley sound so fierce. "I know what I saw."

"So what?"

"So what! Are you crazy?"

"Just take a chill, Ash. It's not a big deal."

"Yes, it is!" Ashley sounded absolutely incensed. "You're wrecking everything!"

"Wrecking everything?" Teagan finally dropped her bored tone and sounded angry. "I'm not the one who wrecked things. Talk to Dad about wrecking things."

You can't blame Dad for — !" Ashley glanced in my direction, saw me and stopped dead. "Jane." She forced a twisted smile. "I didn't see you there."

"I just got here. I wanted to talk to you about the game."

"The game?" Ashley swallowed hard. "What about it?"

"Well, I wanted to say that you were great, that's all. What a goalie! Mr. Jim should put you in first string."

Ashley relaxed. "Oh, I don't know. Sarah's good. But I'm glad I could help us win." Teagan grunted something and walked away as the bell rang. Ashley ignored her. "Come on, let's go to class."

"I have to stop at the CTS room first. I need to ask about extra assignments."

"How come?" Ashley started down the hall.

"Remember the cookie disaster? Well, now I'm practically flunking Foods. So I thought I'd better ask if I can make up the grade somehow."

"Oh." Ashley came with me, and we both stopped in shock at the open classroom door. The CTS room was littered with papers, every drawer and cupboard door was open, and Ms. Horvath was searching feverishly through her desk, scattered pens and worksheets everywhere.

"Um, Ms. Horvath?" I asked tentatively. "Is something wrong?"

Ms. Horvath looked up, wild-eyed. "Jane, you were in class last Friday. The fundraising money from all the pizza and doughnut sales was in an envelope in my desk. Do you remember seeing it anywhere?"

"N-n-no," I stammered. "I don't think so."

"It was in a large, brown envelope. Are you sure you didn't see it?"

I shook my head.

Ms. Horvath exhaled. "I'm sorry, girls. I don't have time to see you right now." She straightened, tucking stray wisps of hair behind her ears. "I need to talk to the principal." She walked toward the door, shooed us out and closed it behind her. She strode off down the hall, the heels of her shoes making determined clicks as she walked.

"What was that all about?" Ashley asked.

"I don't know." I stared down the hall after Ms. Horvath.

"We're going to be late." Ashley nudged my elbow.

"Huh? Oh, yeah. Let's go." We hurried to our lockers, but for the rest of the morning, I thought about Ms. Horvath's messy classroom. Just before lunch I was in gym with Karianne and Ashley when the PA system crackled to life.

"Would Teagan Petrie please report to the office? That's Teagan Petrie to the office, please."

"What'd your sister do now, Ashley? Get arrested?" Karianne joked, but there was an edge in her voice I didn't like.

"Ha-ha. Very funny," I said. Then I noticed that Ashley's lips had gone white. I stopped tossing the dodgeballs into the bin. "Are you okay?" I asked.

"What?" Ashley blinked.

"I said, are you okay?"

"Yeah. Fine. Let's finish up, okay? I'm starved." But Ashley didn't look at me as she said it.

When the bell rang, Ashley bolted out of the gym, not bothering to wait for me. Puzzled, I went to my locker and got my lunch. I'd been eating with Ashley most days since the soccer tryouts, but today she wasn't anywhere to be found. I shrugged to myself and took an empty seat next to some other girls I knew from class, and when Karianne came over and asked if she could sit with me, I nodded yes.

Ashley found me in the lunchroom twenty minutes later. She looked like she was on the verge of tears when she saw me sitting with Karianne. "Jane, can you come with me? I need to talk to you."

"Uh, sure." I stuffed my empty lunch bag in the trash. I could feel Karianne's sharp-eyed gaze follow us as we left.

Ashley steered me toward the nearest girls' room.

"Listen, Ashley. You don't need to be so sensitive about me having lunch with Karianne. I mean, I know she can be a pain in the rear, but she just sat down with me, so it's not like I had much choice —"

"This isn't about Karianne," Ashley cut in. "It's about Teagan."

I felt bewildered. "What about Teagan?"

"Jane, she just got suspended. The police are there and everything." Ashley's tears overflowed.

I gaped at her. "They call the police if you get suspended?"

Ashley sniffled and shook her head. "No. They call them if you're caught stealing from the school."

"What are you talking about?" I heard my voice rising.

"Shhh! Teagan's been stealing money and stuff from open lockers and backpacks, and the teachers figured it out. She's had a few warnings, but no one could prove she did it for sure."

"But you know she did?"

Ashley nodded miserably. "And now they think she stole the fundraising money from the CTS room. That's almost two hundred dollars! I don't think Teagan would take that much."

"Why was she stealing in the first place?" I tried to think reasonably.

"I don't know. She's been weird about money since …." Ashley stopped and bit her lip.

"Since when? It's okay, I won't tell anyone."

She took a deep breath. "Since my mom and dad split up last summer. That's why we moved, because my mom couldn't afford to keep the house we were living in. So we have this gross townhouse near the gas station, and Tee and I had to change schools."

"Okay," I said cautiously.

"But we don't have much money. Not like we used to. My mom's paycheque barely covers what we need."

"Isn't your dad paying child support?" I know about that because of Joey. His mom pays us each month, because he lives with us.

"Not much. He's not making much this year. He has his own store, and business isn't good."

"So what does Teagan have to do with this?"

"She wants the stuff she used to have. She wants an allowance and clothes and makeup and fancy shampoo. She talks all the time about how much she hates being poor."

"You're not poor. Poor is starving to death."

"Tell that to Teagan. She thinks that if Dad stayed, things would be better. She hates him for leaving, and she says nobody cares what she does, anyway."

"So what happened at the office?"

"I went down there, and I saw her with the police officers. They were all talking, and the principal said she was suspended for a week, and they were considering pressing charges." Ashley gulped. "She's only fourteen. They won't throw her in jail, will they?"

"I don't know," I said. I felt helpless. Then the bathroom door fell shut with a soft thud. Ashley and I swivelled in alarm, then stared at each other in shock.

Someone had been listening.

7

Accused

W ho was it?" Ashley panicked. "Do you think she heard?"
"No, I doubt it." I was lying. I was sure the person
had heard everything. "Never mind that. What should we do
about Teagan?"

"She might need someone to talk to," Ashley said. "She's
probably scared."

Somehow I doubted that — in fact I would have placed better odds on the police officers being scared of Teagan, but
decided to keep that opinion to myself.

"Let's go up to the office, then. Maybe they'll let you see her."

I followed Ashley into the hall and we crept toward the office
and looked through the door. Most of the kids were either still in the
lunchroom or outside, but the office was buzzing with activity. One
of the two police officers was writing something, while the other
was talking to Teagan. Ms. Horvath was discussing something with
the principal, the principal was trying to get the secretary's attention, and the secretary was answering the phone.

"Psst." Ashley hissed.

Teagan looked up. When she saw Ashley, she frowned. "Go
away!" she mouthed.

Ashley pointed toward Teagan. "You okay?" I saw her form
the words, but she made no sound.

Teagan rolled her eyes, like she couldn't believe anybody
could be so stupid. "No. Go away," she mouthed again.

"Come on," I whispered. I tugged on Ashley's sleeve. "She probably doesn't want you to see all this." It was the only human trait I'd picked up in Teagan so far.

Ashley let me lead her away. "I don't know what to do," she said.

"Go to class, I guess. Teagan got herself into this mess, she'll have to get herself out."

Ashley sighed. "I can't believe she would steal money from the school."

I didn't answer. I wasn't sure what Teagan would do. From the way she looked and acted though, I would guess she was capable of just about anything.

* * *

"All right, people!" Mrs. Capshaw, our Social Studies teacher, finished handing out newspapers to each group and wiped her newsprint-stained fingers on a paper towel. "Today's current-events assignment is to read each section of the newspaper, cut out articles and group them according to whether they relate to our city, province, country or world. Pick out one story from each pile that you believe is the most important and write a paragraph to explain why."

I turned to face my group, which luckily was pretty good. It was made up of Ashley, Nicholas Garvey from Foods and Jennie Brewster. Jennie was a competitive figure skater — she didn't have much time for homework after school, so she really worked hard in class.

Jennie unfolded the newspaper. "How about we each take a section?"

"I get sports," I said quickly.

"Hey! No fair," Nicholas said.

"She said it first," Jennie said. "Here, Nicholas. You can take the city section instead." She handed him the sheets, and got a wry frown in return.

Ashley took the front section and Jennie settled back with entertainment. I flipped slowly through the sports pages, reading a bit of each article to see which pile it would go in, and whether I thought it was important. On page three, I stopped. There was a photo of a young woman holding speed skates. She was dressed in a hooded spandex outfit, smiling directly at the camera with her parents and younger sister by her side. I glanced down at the caption. Deirdre Phipps, with parents Rob and Eileen and sister Karianne, is tagged as Canada's next Olympic gold-medal hope.

My jaw dropped. That was Karianne's sister! I started reading the article.

Deirdre Phipps has paved her way to the Worlds with a path of gold. In recent years, Phipps placed first in her age category at the Nationals three times and took home a gold in the 1000-metre speed-skating event at the Commonwealth Games. At only seventeen, this skater is one to watch for at the 2006 Olympic Games.

"Wow!" I whispered. "Ashley, look at this."

Ashley seemed to be having a hard time concentrating, for which I could hardly blame her. She hadn't moved past the front page. I thrust the sports pages under her nose. "Look."

Ashley's eyes widened at the photo. "That's Karianne."

"I know. That's her *sister*."

Ashley read the story. "That's amazing. I can't believe she never talks about this. I would, if it was my sister." A trace of bitterness flashed across her face. "Too bad my sister enjoys doing things that I'd rather not brag about."

"You don't know yet if she stole the money for sure," I whispered.

"Does it matter? By the end of the day the whole school will think she did."

"Girls," Mrs. Capshaw said. "Quiet down, please."

I went back to the newspaper and began clipping out each article carefully with scissors. I already knew which one I would choose as the most important. I finished the job quickly, and wrote a paragraph underneath Jennie's about Deirdre Phipps, and how it was an important article because she was from Calgary, but also because she was the sister of someone in our school.

"Boys and girls, it's almost time for the bell. Please put any newsprint you didn't use in the recycling box by the door, and finish this assignment for homework. Don't forget, go to your homeroom teacher to pick up your report cards before dismissal."

Half the class groaned, me included. I'd forgotten it was report card day.

The bell rang. I gathered up my stuff and moved into the hall, almost bumping into Karianne.

"Hey!" I smiled at her. "Guess what? I saw your picture in the paper."

"You did?"

"Yeah. It was a picture of you standing with your parents and your sister. I never knew your sister was a famous athlete. That's so cool, Karianne!"

"Yeah. It's great." Karianne's voice was expressionless.

"It must be really exciting, getting to go to big competitions with her and meeting famous people and stuff."

"I'm not the athlete, Jane. My sister is." Karianne said stonily. "I don't do any of those things."

"Oh. Well…" I hesitated. "I just thought, you know … it's pretty cool, that's all."

Karianne shifted her books and turned away. "I gotta go. See you at the game later."

I stared after her. What was wrong with *her*?

8

Making the Grade

Jane, I don't know what to say." My stepdad stared at the beige folder that held my report card. He'd come home early from work to drive me to my soccer game, and I figured I had a better chance tackling him with the bad news than I would with my mother.

"I do. Try, 'You're grounded!'" Joey was home from school early and on his way to the refrigerator for a snack.

"Butt out, Joe," I said.

"Well, that's what he says to me whenever I give him my report card."

"That's not true," Dad said automatically. "I only said that once." He turned back to me. "Jane, I can't believe you received a failing grade in Home Ec."

"Foods," I corrected.

"Whatever. You love to cook. Some of these other grades could stand improvement, but the home ec one takes the cake."

"No pun intended." Joey sat down at the kitchen table beside me with a box of crackers, a jar of peanut butter, two bananas and a tub of strawberry yogurt.

"Don't you have homework or something?" I said irritably.

"Nope." Joey shoved a cracker smeared with peanut butter into his mouth.

"I'm failing Foods because my teacher hates me."

"She doesn't hate you," Dad said.

"She thinks I'm a total dork."

"That doesn't mean anything. I think you're a total dork, and I don't hate you," Joey said.

I glared at him.

Dad frowned. "Out." He pointed toward the family room.

"Janey knows I was just kidding."

"I know, but — out. I need to talk to Jane. Take your snack in there."

"Your snack that could feed the whole of Ethiopia," I muttered.

Joey grumbled as he gathered his groceries. "I'll leave crumbs on the carpet. Mom hates that."

"I'll risk it. Besides, vacuuming is your job this week." Dad turned back to the report card. I sat still, letting him read the comments. "Jane, I'm not thrilled with your Language Arts mark, and Social Studies could do with some extra work, but you've never failed anything before. Why Home Ec?"

I shrugged. "I told you, Ms. Horvath thinks I'm an idiot."

"No teacher thinks that. Are you fooling around in class?"

"No. I just … well, she makes us do everything exactly by the recipe, with exactly the right measurements and exactly the right tools."

"Tools? Since when do you need tools in Home Ec?" Dad asked.

"Exactly," I said.

"Since Jane started cooking, I've seen her in the kitchen stirring pancakes with a wrench," Joey said on his way back to the refrigerator.

I gritted my teeth. "That was a screwdriver, and I was using it to punch a hole in the box of pancake mix."

"Never mind." Dad said impatiently. "Jane, you do realize you need to pass this course. It's not as though you can drop it."

"I know."

"So, the teacher makes you do everything by the book. What's wrong with that?" Dad asked.

"I don't cook like that. I like to experiment. Why can't I use a cheese grater to get the yellow peel off a lemon? Why can't I use the back of a spoon to smash garlic?" I asked.

"I don't know. Why can't you?"

"Because she makes us use a lemon zester and a garlic press. We're supposed to memorize all this junk, and it's useless. And then I get in trouble if I try to do things differently."

Dad leaned back in his chair. "Your teacher is probably trying to show you how to use the proper utensils."

"Yeah, well, proper isn't fun." I scowled. "I'm a good cook, Dad. The boys eat everything I make. I *like* cooking. But not at school."

"Cooking is cooking, no matter where you are."

"No, it's not. And I've made mistakes, like when I broke the eggs when I was trying to separate them, and when I used too much flour in a batch of ginger cookies, and when I forgot my homework a few times, so now Ms. Horvath thinks I'm a goof-off."

"Have you tried talking to her?"

"I was going to go in and ask for some extra assignments to pull up my grade, but she didn't have time to see me."

"What!" Dad looked angry at that.

"No, it really was important." I explained about the missing money.

"Did you go back later to talk to her?"

"No." I looked down at the table. "She really doesn't like me, Dad. It's hard enough being in class. I guess I just didn't want to."

Dad patted my shoulder. "I know. But you have to. Just picture her as an opposing soccer player. You wouldn't hesitate to deal with her then, would you?"

"That's totally different!"

"No, it's not. They're both people who are challenging you."

"Dad, you don't understand *anything*," I said in exasperation.

"I understand one thing. The rule in this house is grades come before sports. I'm sorry, Janey, but if you don't deal with this Home-Ec grade, Mom and I will have to pull you from the soccer team."

"That's not fair!" I said in alarm. "It's Foods, for Pete's sake. It's not like I'm failing Math or something."

"I know." Dad looked uncomfortable. I knew for a fact he thought soccer was more important than a cooking course. "But you know what Mom is going to say. You're still failing a course, and some of these other marks need attention. I'm not saying you have to stop soccer right now …."

"Mom will." My mother was very firm about our grades.

"I'll try to talk her out of it. But don't just piddle around, okay? Go and see this teacher and get this mark up. Okay?"

"Okay," I said glumly.

"Better pack up your gear and get changed. Your game starts in an hour."

I hustled upstairs, tossed my jeans over my desk chair and pulled on my soccer shorts, shin pads and socks. Dry grass fell from the velcro of the shin pads — leftovers from the last game — and littered the carpet. Stepping over that, I reached for a clean t-shirt to wear under my jersey. It was still kind of cold outside, and an extra shirt would come in handy.

"Come on, Jane!" Dad hollered from downstairs. "Let's go!"

"Just a sec!" I pulled on my jersey, stuffed my jacket and water bottle into my soccer bag and grabbed my cleats. I rushed downstairs in my sock-feet to the front door.

"Ready?" Dad was jingling his keys when I returned. I yanked on my cleats and we left.

The field was busy when we pulled up. Several games were being played, and I had to look for my team colours to see which field we were on. I got out of the car and shivered, pulling on my jacket.

"Hi, Jane," Mr. Jim greeted me. "Start stretching out, and then run a few laps. You're on first shift."

I sat down next to Ashley. "Hey," I said.

"Hi." Ashley looked glum.

"How's Teagan?"

"Well, she's not in jail."

"That's good news."

Ashley snorted. "I guess. The whole school knows she's suspended, though. They know about the missing money, too. I've had about twenty people ask me about it already. Like I'd know!"

"Don't worry. It'll be okay."

Ashley glanced at me, her eyes hard. "Yeah, right. For who?" She got up and began running laps around the field.

I tried not to feel hurt. I knew Ashley was mad at her sister, and I knew she was embarrassed. I stretched my leg muscles harder and shook them out. Right now, I had a game to play. That was the only thing I wanted to focus on.

I started my laps, running slowly at first, then building up speed. I ran hard for half the field, then slowed, then sprinted again. I wanted to get my heart rate up without losing too much stamina before the game.

Mr. Jim blew his whistle, beckoning the team to come in.

"Okay, ladies. We've started the season well — let's keep the winning streak going. I've seen some excellent teamwork in practice. Let's take it into the game. Okay? Let's go!"

I trotted out on to the field with the rest of the first shift. We didn't have enough players to make two full shifts, so we had to really watch for when Mr. Jim signalled us off.

The Jaguars were a good team. I sized up their striker as I shook out my legs and took a deep breath. She was taller than me and looked like she might be really fast. I knew I'd have to be quick if I was going to get the ball away from her.

When the ref blew the whistle to start the game, I slashed out with one foot and deked sideways. Both my other forwards were struggling to get in the clear, so I faked out the Jags' striker and sprinted as far down the field as I could get. The mid-fielders, taken a little by surprise by this aggressive approach, clustered ahead of me to stop the ball. I checked over my shoulder and saw my forward open to the right. I aimed a pass, but one of their players scooped it up and raced into our defence. I hustled back, but stayed far enough behind that I could take a pass if I needed to. I watched Ashley marshalling our defence as sweeper, and Sarah crouched at the ready in goal.

The Jags' passes were crisp and clean. Our defence was having trouble intercepting as the ball worked its way closer to our goal.

Suddenly their striker trapped the ball and took a shot, aiming for the far corner of the net. Sarah dove for the ball. Her fingers just tipped it in mid-air and it spun away from the goal post. Sarah landed sideways on the ground, skidding on the muddy patch in front of the goal where the grass was worn thin.

"Way to go, Sarah!" I yelled.

Sarah jumped up, her gloves, shorts and kneepads covered in mud. She didn't bother to brush herself off, but immediately crouched into her goalie stance.

Our defence was all over the ball this time. By now, the Jags' mid-fielders were down in the zone, and it was beginning to look like a game of keep-away.

"Heads up, Jane!" Karianne hollered. She tried to send a long pass to me, but the Jags' striker moved like lightning and had the ball before I could even move in on it.

This time the defence had no chance to even force a pass. The Jags' striker sprinted around them all and moved in for a beautiful goal. Sarah dove and almost grasped the ball, but it sailed through her gloves and into the net. I was right — that striker *was* fast — and now we were down one point.

Sarah smacked her hands together, shaking off clods of mud. A second dive had left her gloves plastered with it. She motioned to Mr. Jim, and he called for a time-out. I jogged over to the bench and grabbed my water bottle, even though I'd hardly broken a sweat.

"Okay, girls," Mr. Jim said. "This team is obviously strong offensively. We need our defence to tighten up. Expect a passing game from them. Cover them hard, make sure they can't work in a pass. Sarah can't do it all here. Keep that striker covered, in particular. Jane, Emily and Jen, I need you three to work the ball forward — let's see if their defence is as tough as their offense."

"Mr. Jim?" Sarah stepped forward, a perplexed look on her face. "My spare gloves are missing."

Mr. Jim looked up. "What?"

"My spare gloves. They were in my bag, but now they're gone. I can't play with these." She held up her soggy, mud-soaked gloves. "They're too slippery. I can't keep hold of the ball. That's why I just cost us a goal."

Mr. Jim scratched his head. "Has anyone seen Sarah's gloves?"

All the girls shook their heads.

"Does anyone have a spare pair? Ashley?" Mr. Jim looked at her hopefully.

"I...uh...don't have a pair," Ashley said in a small voice.

"Great," Mr. Jim muttered. "My backup goalie doesn't have her equipment, and we have a kleptomaniac loose on the team."

"Well, doesn't that just add up to two and two," Karianne said under her breath. Her face was very white.

"What's that supposed to mean?" I demanded.

"Think about it. Someone's sister just got nailed for stealing at school. Hmm, who could that be? And that same person doesn't even have her own equipment — equipment that just went missing. Sound a little suspicious?"

Ashley's face had turned a mottled purple. "Shut up, Karianne!"

"Hey, now!" Mr. Jim put up his hands.

Ashley blinked back tears. "I'm not like my sister! I wouldn't steal anything!" But she wouldn't meet anyone's gaze, not even mine.

Karianne looked skeptical. Emily, Jen and the rest of the

team kept glancing at each other, questions in their eyes. I watched Ashley, but she wouldn't look up.

Sarah was angry. "Geez, Ashley. I would have let you borrow them if you needed them."

Ashley gave a strangled gulp. "I didn't do it!" She struggled not to cry.

Mr. Jim frowned. "We don't know what happened, and you can't go accusing people of stealing without proof, Karianne. We're in the middle of a game here. This discussion can wait.

So let's re-focus on the game, and give it everything you have. We need this one, girls."

But no one played well after that. We lost abysmally. You could see that Ashley wasn't concentrating. Sarah was playing with slick gloves that let even the easy shots get by. And I couldn't get rid of the image of Ashley staring down at the ground after Karianne accused her, refusing to look me in the eye.

9

Food Fight

Karianne was careful not to talk about soccer in Foods the next day, but just being around her was making me angry. "So, do you want to peel the carrots?" she asked.

"I'll do the potatoes." I lifted my chin, but Karianne didn't object. The assignment today was to make a health-conscious dinner, with fish or chicken, potatoes or rice, and a vegetable. Nicholas was absent, so Karianne and I had to do all three.

"Better put the chicken in the oven first," Karianne advised, looking at the instructions, which she wasn't letting me anywhere near. "It takes the longest to cook."

I slapped the raw chicken in a glass casserole dish. "Now what?"

Karianne pretended not to notice my attitude. She consulted the recipe. "Cover with two teaspoons of olive oil, sprinkle with rosemary, and bake at 375 degrees for half an hour."

I found the oil and the spice and complied, then shoved the dish in the oven.

"You were probably supposed to pre-heat that," Karianne said.

"Who cares?" I said testily, twisting the oven knobs on. I turned to Karianne, who was rinsing carrots in the sink.

"You know," I began. "That wasn't fair, saying that Ashley stole that stuff. You had no right."

"Get real." Karianne snorted. "It's obvious." She concentrated on the carrot she was peeling.

"Why? Just because her sister's got a bad reputation?" I demanded.

"More like her sister's got a record. Teagan got suspended for stealing, Jane. That's not just a bad reputation. Plus Ashley's stuff is total garbage. The only thing that looks decent is her jersey, and that's because the team gives them out. Haven't you noticed her bashed-up cleats? Her faded shorts and socks that are full of holes? Do you think it's, like, coincidence that some of our equipment is going missing? Why would anybody else steal it? Who would have a reason?"

I didn't want to admit it, but she did have a point. Ashley had told me about how Teagan started stealing because she was angry that her family didn't have the money they used to have. What if Ashley felt the same way, but didn't want to tell me? Maybe she didn't care about the same things Teagan cared about, but I knew soccer was important to her. Maybe she was embarrassed about having not having the money for good equipment.

Karianne had been watching my face. "See?" she said. "It's possible, isn't it?"

"That doesn't mean it's true," I retorted.

Karianne started peeling carrots with vigour. I scrubbed the potatoes with the vegetable brush, instead of using a sponge like I would at home. Ms. Horvath was still across the room, helping another group, but I wanted to make a good impression on her with this assignment. I still had to talk to her about making up my grade.

"What's that smell?" Karianne looked up.

"What smell?"

"Something smells funny."

I sniffed. "Like smoke." I turned to see greyish wisps escaping from the oven door. "Augh! The chicken's on fire!" I leaped to the stove and wrenched open the door. Smoke poured out, and the chicken was flickering with orange flames. In a panic, I reached for the fire extinguisher — there was one attached to the side of every counter. I pulled the pin.

"Jane, *no!*" Ms. Horvath was running from the other side of the room.

Too late. Foam spewed everywhere — into the oven, over the chicken, onto the floor. It splattered the counters. A horrible, acrid smell rose from the oven.

Ms. Horvath slid on the foam as she reached our station. Regaining her balance, she pulled off her dress shoes and stood there in her nylons. "Hand me the oven mitts," she commanded. I gave them to her meekly.

Ms. Horvath pulled the blackened pan of chicken, now topped liberally with white foam, from the oven and set it on the stove. Then she reached for the oven controls.

"Which one of you is responsible for turning this oven on?" she asked.

"Jane," Karianne said promptly.

"I should have guessed." Ms. Horvath turned to me. "Jane. We discussed how an oven works in the first week of classes. Do you remember that?"

I nodded, a lump in my throat.

"Well, then. Surely you recall that we discussed the broiler function, and how we *do not use it* unless a teacher specifically tells you to, because it gets very, very hot. I'm sure we also covered how, when food is left under the broiler for an extended period of time, it tends to catch on fire. Do you remember that?"

I swallowed. "Yes," I whispered.

"Can you tell me, then, why this oven is on broil, not bake?"

"I didn't mean to. I made a mistake."

Ms. Horvath sighed heavily. "Jane, you make far too many mistakes in this class." She surveyed the mess around her. "I appreciate the fact that you acted quickly in trying to put out the fire, but turning off the broiler and keeping the oven closed would have been far less messy. I'll have to ask you to stay behind and clean this up. I'll let your teacher know that you'll be missing class. The rest of you, please finish up. Karianne, you may join group one's assignment, and I'll grade you with them."

The class moved away, and Ms. Horvath studied me with an expression like granite. "There are rags and cleanser under the sink."

"Uh ... Ms. Horvath?" My voice quavered. "I was wondering if I could do some make-up assignments to pull up my grade."

Ms. Horvath's cheek twitched. "Jane, I don't think either the school or my nerves could afford it. And at this point, it wouldn't make much difference. You'd have to get top marks, and I think we both know you're not capable of that in here."

I looked down, blinking back tears. I *was* capable. I just couldn't seem to prove it to this teacher. But somehow I would. Maybe my dad was right. I never backed down from a challenge on the field — so why should I start in cooking class?

10

Playing Games

The ball smacked hard against the inside of my foot and spun away.

"Control, Jane. Concentrate on stopping the ball," Mr. Jim yelled from the middle of the field. I felt my face flush and chased after it. We were working on practice drills before the start of the next game, and Mr. Jim had already stressed that we really needed to be on top of things if we were going to win this one.

I looked for Ashley so we could partner up, but she was nowhere on the field. I spotted her at the sidelines. I figured she'd stopped for a drink, and that sounded good to me, too. I jogged in her direction.

Ashley had her back to me and was bending down, pawing through the pile of soccer bags. She had something in her hand.

I cleared my throat. "Ash?"

Ashley swivelled around. "Jane! Is practice over?"

"Not yet." I eyed the object in her hand curiously. Ashley quickly tucked her hand in the pocket of her shorts. "What are you doing?" I asked.

"I ... uh ... just needed something from my bag."

"Your bag's over here by the bench, next to mine."

"Right. Yeah. Good." Ashley moved toward it and fumbled with the zipper. "You go on. I'll be right there."

"Okay." But I moved only a little way off. I narrowed my eyes as Ashley took whatever-it-was out of the pocket of her shorts and deposited it in her bag. Then she joined me. We only had time for a few passes before Mr. Jim signalled us to come to the centre of the field.

"Good work, girls. I've seen some nice improvement. Keep focused, and we'll have this game nailed." Mr. Jim smiled at us.

I put out my hand. "Team cheer, guys!" The rest of the girls put their hands on top of mine. "One, two, three, *gooooooooooooo* Hurricanes!" We broke the circle and everyone ran for the sidelines, except me. I grabbed the bag of practice balls and lugged it in, dumping it near the rest of our gear. Then I sat down and began to stretch out my legs. I wanted keep limber and warm for the start of the game.

Emily, who had been stretching nearby, sat beside me and unlaced her cleats. She rummaged through her bag. She stopped, looking puzzled, and then did it again.

"I can't find my other shin pads," Emily said.

"What's wrong with the ones you have?" I asked, pausing mid-stretch.

"The velcro strap broke on the field." Emily yanked down her sock to show me, then continued to search. "I know I had them in my bag."

The team fell silent. Emily chewed on her lip. Nobody looked at Ashley.

"The refs won't let you play without shin pads. Are you sure they're not there?" I said.

Emily dumped it upside down. Her water bottle, jacket, running shoes, hair brush and a pair of sweatpants rained down, but no shin pads. "They're gone."

I glanced up. Ashley had the look of a deer poised to flee. She stared at me with scared eyes.

Karianne was frowning. Before she could say anything, I started shuffling bags around. "Let's look a little harder. They've got to be here somewhere."

Karianne started helping me move the soccer bags and jackets aside, and Sarah and Emily joined in. Sarah started checking any bags that were unzipped, in case the shin pads had been put somewhere accidently. I lifted the bag full of practice balls and saw a flash of white beneath them.

"Here they are!" I held them up in triumph. I could see the relief flooding Ashley's face. "You must have taken them out of your bag, Em, and put them on the grass. I didn't see them when I dragged the practice balls over here."

"Thanks, Jane." Emily started to remove her socks.

I exhaled. I hadn't realized I'd been holding my breath. "Good. So everything's okay, then."

"Not quite." Sarah said. She had a shocked look on her face.

I whirled around. "What's the matter?"

"My kneepads are gone and I have a wicked bruise from last game. I can't play in goal without them."

"Did you … leave them somewhere?" I asked.

"No. They were in my bag. The bag was zipped." Sarah's voice was flat. She shot an angry look at Ashley.

"I didn't take them," Ashley said defiantly.

"Nobody said you did," Karianne shot back. "So why are you so touchy all of a sudden?"

"Because you're all thinking that I did!" Ashley retorted. "But I wouldn't steal anything, I swear! Just because my sister did, doesn't mean I would. Tell them, Jane!" Ashley turned to me.

I opened my mouth to speak. But then I remembered the things Karianne had said. *Haven't you noticed her bashed-up cleats? Her faded shorts and socks that are full of holes? Do you think it's any coincidence that some of our equipment is going missing? Why would anybody else steal it? Who would have a reason?* I hesitated. Ashley *had* been acting strangely, searching through the bags in the middle of practice.

Ashley's eyes filled with tears. "Fine," she said, her voice choked. "If that's what you believe, then I'm gone." She picked up her bag and walked away.

Everyone stared after her, but no one said a word. She was more than halfway down the field when Mr. Jim came back from the parking lot, lugging the extra-large thermos of Thirst-Ade for halftime, which he had gone to get from his car.

He gave us a puzzled look. "What's going on? Where's Ashley?"

I took a deep breath. "I think she just quit the team."

11

Teagan Talks

I stood outside the row of shabby townhouses for a long time, gearing up my nerve. I was going to be late for soccer practice if I didn't hurry.

I'd followed Ashley home. Since I'd never been to her place, it was lucky for me that she walked back and forth to school. That way it had been easy to follow her and find out where she lived.

I couldn't think of any other way to talk to her. For the last three days, she wouldn't answer the phone, and she refused to talk to me at school. I wasn't even sure she would answer the door, but I had no other plan.

"You waiting for a bus?" The curt voice behind me caused me to jump. I turned and saw Teagan. "'Cause I got news for you. It stops down the street."

Teagan looked more subdued than usual. She was wearing jeans with a black sweatshirt and big gold hoop earrings, and her hair was an array of messy spikes.

"I ... uh ... wanted to talk to Ashley," I said.

"So what's stopping you?" Teagan asked. She shifted the wad of gum in her mouth and blew a bubble.

"I'm not sure she wants to talk to me," I admitted.

Teagan frowned and hooked one thumb through the belt loop of her jeans. "Why not?"

"You don't know?"

"Ash doesn't tell me anything."

I shuffled my feet. "Some of the girls think Ashley's the one who's been stealing stuff from our team."

Teagan was silent.

"Ashley asked me to stick up for her — and I didn't. I just wasn't sure, after … well —"

"I got suspended," Teagan finished. She didn't sound angry, just matter-of-fact.

"Yeah. And then she quit."

"Ash quit the soccer team?" The surprise in Teagan's voice was genuine.

"She hasn't been to practice for three days," I said.

Teagan chomped on her gum. "What're you gonna tell her?"

"I'm … I'm not sure, exactly," I faltered.

"You still think Ashley stole that stuff?" Teagan's eyes narrowed dangerously.

I wondered whether to say what I was thinking, then decided to be honest. "One of the girls on the team said that Ashley's equipment is always so old and beat up. I wondered if maybe … she wished her things were better. Some money went missing once, too."

Teagan scowled. "I took the money. And Ashley found the wallet in my jacket and tried to give it back."

"She did?" I was startled. Maybe that explained why I found her rummaging through the bags on the bench during practice.

"Yeah."

"What about Sarah's cleats and the other equipment?"

Teagan shook her head. "I don't know anything about that. I didn't touch it." Teagan thought for a minute. "Sarah's the goalie, right? The short girl with the curly, brown hair?"

"Yeah," I said cautiously.

"What size shoes does she wear?"

I felt confused by this weird question. "How should I know? Maybe a six. Her feet are pretty small," I answered.

"Well, Ash wears a nine. She's always complaining that her feet are huge. So why would she take Sarah's cleats?" Teagan gave me a triumphant smile.

"I'm glad," I said. "I never wanted to think Ashley would ever steal."

"She doesn't."

"So why do you?" I asked point-blank.

Teagan's smile faded. "I don't know. Because."

"Because why?" I persisted.

Teagan looked uncomfortable. "Money, why else?"

"You could get a job. You're old enough."

"I know." Teagan seemed to be searching for the right words. "But that's too normal. Then my parents would think everything is okay."

"And it's not?"

Teagan gritted her teeth. "My dad left last summer. It was like, "see ya," and that was it. I think that stinks. And my mom is always working now, she's never home —" Teagan broke off. "I hate it. We had to move out of our house, my parents still fight about money all the time. Ashley had to beg my mom for the cash for her soccer fees … we even recycled cans to get the money together … I told Ashley I'd get her the money, but she wouldn't take it. She knew where I was getting it even though I never told her. So you can tell your fancy friends on the soccer team that they're a bunch of losers. Ashley would never steal."

"But then …." I stopped as another thought occurred to me. I stared at Teagan. "But if Ashley didn't steal the equipment … then who did?"

12

Ashley's Big Idea

I marched up to Ashley at school the next day. Teagan had said it might be better if she talked to Ashley first, so I went to soccer practice yesterday without trying to see her.

"Ashley?"

No answer. She kept riffling through her notebook, her locker door open.

"I know you didn't steal anything." I said quietly. "I should have told the rest of the team that. I'm really sorry."

Ashley still stared at her open notebook, but I saw her chin wobbling.

"Ashley, you have to come back to the team. We really need you."

"Why should I? Even if you don't think I took all that stuff, everyone else does."

"So what? We just have to prove you didn't," I said.

"How?"

"Maybe by catching the person who did."

Ashley snorted. "Give me a break, Jane."

"What? You think we can't? Okay, well … I just thought soccer meant a lot to you. But never mind. Just because Karianne is playing goal now, and she totally stinks, is no reason for you to come back, I guess. See ya." I started to turn away.

"Wait." Ashley caught my elbow. "What do you mean, Karianne's playing goal?"

"Sarah twisted her knee in practice yesterday," I said. "Mr. Jim had to use Karianne, and, man, is she awful. I don't know how she managed to play goal last year without getting booted off the team."

I saw Ashley's lips twitch in a reluctant smile. "She can't be that bad."

"She is," I said emphatically. "We need you."

Ashley's smile fell. "I can't come back, Jane. I want to. I miss playing a lot. But nobody trusts me."

"If we find the real thief, they will."

"We'll never be able to do that."

"Why not?" I asked.

"Because … life isn't like a bad TV show, that's why not."

"Think, Ashley. Somebody has been taking equipment. Not just once, but three times. Why? Why did they do it? Maybe they'll do it again, and we can catch them in the act."

I could see Ashley wavering. "Mr. Jim might not let me come back."

"You've only missed one practice and two games. Tell him what's going on. He'll understand."

"I walked off in the middle of a game, though," Ashley said doubtfully.

"Trust me, he'll want you back. Especially when he finds out I might have to quit."

Ashley's eyes widened. "You're quitting? Why?"

"Ms. Horvath won't let me do any extra work to make up the assignments I messed up. I'm failing Foods, and my parents won't let me play soccer if I flunk a course."

"Even if it's Foods?" Ashley looked horrified.

I nodded. "Completely lame, isn't it?"

"Why won't Ms. Horvath let you make up the grade?"

"Because she thinks I'm a kitchen loser."

"But that's not fair!" Ashley said. "You're an awesome cook! I tasted that stuff you brought for lunch ages ago. You're terrific!"

"Tell that to Ms. Horvath," I said glumly. "For some reason, I just can't do anything right in her class. She makes me nervous, watching me all the time, making sure I follow every rule. Sometimes I'd like to take her dumb measuring cups and throw them out the window."

Ashley tried to grin at that, but couldn't quite. "You have to stay on the soccer team with me, Jane. Everyone else thinks I'm some weird klepto who lifts used soccer gear. I can't go back without you."

"Yeah, well … I have to pass Foods first. If you think trying to catch a thief is hard, try passing a CTS course with Ms. Horvath!"

* * *

Karianne was a bigger pain than usual. In Foods, she kept going on about how the team would have a better chance now that she was in goal, until I nearly wanted to barf. She seemed so happy, though. It was hard to believe that she didn't realize that she just didn't have the skill.

Luckily, we didn't have much time to talk. We had a double period, and Ms. Horvath told us at the beginning of class that we had a quiz at the end of our kitchen assignment, so we couldn't waste any time.

"All right boys and girls," Ms. Horvath stood at the front of the room. "Today we are winding up our baking-basics unit with quick breads. By now you should have mastered this technique, since quick breads are very similar to muffins in composition."

I could already feel my eyes closing. I might actually die of boredom in this class, I thought. Ms. Horvath kept talking, illustrating her points by lifting various utensils, then finally let us get up and get to work.

I checked out our recipe. "Oh, this is so easy. I can practically make banana bread in my sleep," I said.

"Don't try," said Karianne through clenched teeth. "Just keep out of the way. I want to get a good mark on this."

"No, really, Karianne. I can make awesome banana bread." Karianne eyed me doubtfully.

"Seriously. I can." I pulled the blender out from the cupboard.

"What are you going to do with that?" Karianne demanded.

"Make banana bread," I answered.

"No! No way. Do it the way we're supposed to, or forget it," Karianne hissed.

"Trust me." I dumped flour, baking soda and powder, and salt and sugar into the mixing bowl.

"Jane, if you mess this up…" Karianne threatened.

Nicholas leaned against the counter. "Chill out, Karianne."

I plugged the blender in, peeled the overripe bananas and dumped them in with the eggs and some milk. I turned it on. At the noise, Ms. Horvath looked up.

"Jane, what is going on?"

I tried to smile as I scooped the thick paste from the blender into the mixing bowl. "This is an easier way of making banana bread."

"Jane, I didn't ask you to use the blender. I asked you to use the utensils laid out for you." Ms. Horvath fixed me with a steely look.

"I know. But this way you don't get soggy banana lumps in the bread."

Ms. Horvath sighed through her nose. "Karianne and Nicholas, you may start your own batch of banana bread. Jane's will be graded alone." She eyed me, and I could hear her unspoken words, *and it had better be good!*"

But this time I was confident. I'd made this thousands of times, and it always turned out great. I finished scraping the last of the banana mixture out of the blender and added some melted margarine to the bowl. I stirred it up with a few quick strokes and then poured the mixture into greased loaf pans. The oven was already pre-heating, and I stuck the pan in the oven, confident that this time, I'd finally done something right.

The loaves rose up, brown and crusty, and when I took them out, I was sure Ms. Horvath would be impressed.

She finished with group three and moved on to me. She hardly paused. "Better," she said, before moving on to Karianne and Nicholas.

That was it? Wasn't she even going to taste it? Annoyed, I began cleaning up. I clattered the blender parts into the sink, washing with more vigour than necessary. I knew that bread was better than anyone else's in class, and Ms. Horvath just didn't want to admit it. She was so used to thinking of me as a goof-off that she couldn't see me as anything else.

When the bell rang, Karianne followed me out the door but stopped when she saw Ashley waiting for me there.

"What's she doing here?" Karianne hissed at me.

I ignored her and approached Ashley, who had that deer-caught-in-the-headlights look again when she spotted Karianne. "What's up?" I asked.

Ashley forced herself to ignore Karianne and handed me a copy of *TeenWorld* magazine. "Look." She let the magazine fall open to where she had marked the place.

I peered at the headline. "*Soap star Aidan Miles leaving* Sands of Time *for prime time docudrama*. Well, that's interesting and everything, Ash, but I don't think it's worth coming all the way from the library to tell me."

"No, you doof!" Ashley slugged my shoulder. "Look on the other page!"

"Kids' CookFest … over $5000 in prizes. Yeah…so?"

"Hello? Jane … are you in there?" Ashley said. "Think about it. You have to submit an original recipe to the contest. How many kids do you know that cook recipes they make up themselves?"

I shrugged. "I dunno." We started walking down the hall toward my locker.

"Well, I do! Not very many. But you do. You could win this contest, Jane. And then nobody could say you don't know how to cook. Ms. Horvath would *have* to pass you."

"Let me see that." I took the magazine from her and scanned the contest article. "It says you have to be under fourteen, and the grand prize is $1000 educational-fund certificate, plus a $500 dollar shopping spree. Wow. Wouldn't that be great?" I looked a little closer. "It also says that submissions have to be mailed by *tomorrow night*!" I looked at Ashley in dismay. "I can't make something up by tomorrow."

"Why not?" Ashley said. "Use one of the recipes you've already made. Like your spinach bread or something."

I made a face. "Do you really think that the contest judges will like green bread? It has to be something special."

We reached my locker and I spun the combination lock.

"What else have you made?"

"Tons of stuff. But you can hardly call scrambled eggs with tomatoes and cheddar cheese a recipe."

"Why not?" Ashley asked.

"Because it's too easy."

"Easy sounds good, especially for kids."

"Yeah, but like I said, it should be something really special if it's going to win. Brownies or something."

"Brownies would be great."

"Except that I haven't invented any lately." I took out my jacket and backpack.

"Well, let's go to your house and experiment. Want to?"

"Okay." It was hard not to catch Ashley's enthusiasm. I think she was glad to have something else to think about than what had been happening on the team.

When we got to my house, I marched straight to the kitchen. "Okay … everybody out. There's some serious cooking about to happen here."

Trent and Joey looked up from the mega-bag of potato chips

and the vat of dip they were consuming with single-minded dedication. "Do we get to sample the results?" Trent asked.

"If they're edible." I began pulling out cookbooks.

"Wait." Ashley stopped me. "Don't even bother looking in there. We can't use a recipe that's been published, remember?"

"I know. I just wanted to get some ideas."

"Well, ask the experts." Ashley gestured toward my brothers.

"I don't know who your friend is, Janey, but I like her already," Joey said. He wiped his potato-chip-greasy fingers on the back of his jeans, leaned forward and extended his hand. "I'm Joey, and this is Trent."

"I'm Ashley." She actually blushed as she shook Joey's hand.

"So what are you cooking, Janey?" Trent stuffed another potato chip into his mouth.

"I don't know yet. Ashley came up with this idea to enter the *TeenWorld* CookFest. If I win, maybe Ms. Horvath will reconsider flunking me in Foods, and I won't have to quit the soccer team."

"You're flunking Foods?" Trent looked at me in disbelief. "That's, like…impossible."

"Impossible, but true." I found a notebook and a pen for writing down ingredients.

"That's why I thought we should ask you guys," Ashley said. "What's your favourite thing that Jane's ever cooked?"

"That's easy," Trent said. "Nachos, for sure."

"No way," Joey argued. "Her omelettes are way better."

Adam stuck his head in the kitchen. "What's going on?"

"What's your favorite thing Janey's cooked for you?" Trent asked.

"Mmm … chili, maybe."

"Yeah, her chili rocks," Joey agreed.

"Geez, how much cooking do you do?" Ashley turned to me.

"With these bottomless pits? Too much." I shook my head.

"Hey, I know something that would be good for the contest.

Man, they were terrific. And I bet no one has ever made them like you did, Janey," Joey said.

"Great. Do you feel like explaining what it is?" I was getting testy, with this crowd hanging around.

"Remember those strawberry muffins you made a few months ago? With that strawberry butter? They were awesome." Joey rubbed his stomach.

"Yeah, they were," Adam said seriously.

"Okay … I'll admit, those have to be at least as good as her nachos," Trent said.

"But … I don't remember how to make them!" I wailed. "I only made them once, and I didn't have a recipe."

"But that's perfect!" Ashley exclaimed. "It's an original recipe, then."

"Yeah!" I said sarcastically. "If I knew what it was!"

"We'll just re-create it. You can do it, Jane. I know you can," Ashley said.

"I guess I can try." I began pulling out mixing bowls and muffin tins.

"And you know," Trent patted my shoulder encouragingly. "We're here to help you dispose of the failures."

I raised my eyebrows at him. "Good thing there's a lot of Gas-Eeze in the house."

13

Jane's Creative Kitchen

"Joey is totally cute." Ashley leaned against the counter.

"He thinks so, anyway." I shook my head, wiping potato-chip crumbs off the counter so we had space to work. "Come on. We'd better get to work."

"What should I do?"

"Check in the freezer and see how many strawberries are left in the bag. My mom usually buys them in bulk." I pulled a brick of butter out of the fridge. We'd managed to clear the boys out of the kitchen, and I had at least an hour before Mom or Dad would be home and would need the oven for dinner.

Ashley looked over her shoulder. "It looks like there's about half a bag."

"Good." I handed her a colander. "Put a bunch in here and run them under cold water to get them thawed out a bit."

Ashley dumped a load of whole strawberries into the container. "Whoops. Is that too many?"

I eyed the amount. "Yeah. Take out about half. I usually make double batches of everything, because the boys gobble it up so fast, but I don't want to waste too much if I mess up."

"You won't," Ashley said confidently. "This isn't Food Studies. This is Jane's Creative Kitchen."

"Yeah, right." I couldn't help laughing.

"Okay, now what?"

I thought for a minute. "I think I probably melted the butter and put it in the blender with the strawberries and the eggs."

"The blender?"

"Yeah. I make lots of stuff with the blender. Saves time."

"Okay," Ashley answered doubtfully. "But the strawberries will be all mushed up."

"That's the point. They *were* mushed up. The muffins turn out pink. If you use pieces of the berry, they make soggy spots in the dough. I tried that once before." I pulled out the crock of flour and a recipe book. "I just want to check how much flour and stuff they use for regular muffins," I said, catching Ashley's look. I began measuring flour, baking soda, baking powder and salt into the big mixing bowl. Then I added some sugar and stirred the mixture around. "Okay, now dump the berries into the blender." I pulled out a carton of eggs, cracked two and tossed them in with the strawberries. Then I thought for a minute, before searching through the fridge.

"What are you looking for?" Ashley asked.

"I think I used yogurt last time." I came up with a carton of low-fat sour cream. "This'll do." I plopped a few spoonfuls into the blender, punched on the lid and turned it on. The berries whirled with the sour cream, eggs and butter, until they made a thick, pink liquid. I unfastened the blender container, popped open the lid and poured the liquid into the bowl of dry ingredients. "Better turn the oven on," I instructed Ashley. "I forgot to pre-heat it."

"Will that matter?" Ashley turned the dial and grabbed a spoon to help me get the last of the pink goop out of the blender.

"I don't think so. By the time we fill the muffin tins, it should be hot enough." I put the blender in the sink and fished a long wooden spoon out of the jug on the counter. "Can you spray the tins with non-stick spray?" I asked. I handed her the canister. Ashley directed a squirt of spray into each muffin holder while I mixed the batter.

"Done." Ashley capped the spray.

"Good. Help me fill the tins, okay? Just use a couple of spoonfuls, and fill each one about three-quarters full. We have to be quick, because muffins rise better if they're baked right away."

Once the tins were full, we slid them into the oven and set the timer for twenty-five minutes. "I'm not sure if that's the right time," I cautioned. "We have to watch and make sure they don't burn."

"Let's write down all the ingredients and how much we used before we forget," Ashley suggested. We sat at the kitchen table and wrote while a delicious scent of warm strawberries rose from the oven.

"What about the strawberry butter Joey told us about?" Ashley asked.

I waved a hand. "That's so easy. It's just strawberry jam and butter whipped together with the mixer."

Ashley jumped up. "Let's make some so we can try it with the muffins. They must be just about done.

I peeked into the oven. "About five more minutes, I think."

"Can I make the strawberry butter?" Ashley asked.

"Sure." I got some jam and the butter and dumped equal amounts into a smaller bowl and handed her the mixer. "Just whip it until it's really smooth."

I listened to the whir of the mixer for a few minutes, then pulled out the muffins. I stuck a toothpick in the middle of a few to see if they were cooked. If the toothpick comes out clean, without dough sticking to it, the muffins are done. "I think they're ready," I said.

"Great. So's the butter." Ashley came over to look. She sniffed. "Mmmm."

"Want one?" I used a knife to gently pry a muffin loose. "They're too hot, but we'd better taste them before the boys get in here."

Ashley found us two plates. I gingerly laid a muffin on each and sliced them open. A gentle steam rose up, and I quickly slathered each half with the butter-and-jam mixture. It melted into the hot muffin, filling the kitchen with the scent of warm, sugared strawberries.

Ashley bit into one and closed her eyes "Mmmmm. These are awesome, Jane," she said. "Contest-winners for sure."

"Let's hope so," I answered.

14

Secret Keeper

I stopped by Karianne's locker after school the next day. She was stuffing homework into her backpack, a new leather jacket looped over one arm.

"Are you going to practice today?" I asked.

She straightened and smiled. "Of course. Are you?"

"Yes." I hesitated. "Ashley's coming back to the team."

Karianne's smile faded. "She is?"

"Yeah."

"Did Mr. Jim say she could come back?"

I nodded. "I know how happy you've been playing goal. I just wanted to let you know that Ashley might get put in."

"Why?" Karianne spat. "Because she's collected enough goalie equipment to finally play a game?"

"No," I said evenly. "Because she's good. And no one can prove that she stole anything. It's not fair to assume she's guilty without proof."

Karianne slammed her locker door shut. "Well, that's just great. How much does she have to steal before she finally gets kicked off?"

"Ashley's not the one who's stealing stuff," I said firmly. "I don't know who is, but it's not her."

Karianne shook her head. "Whatever. I have to go." She hoisted her backpack, which was overflowing with notes, binders and several library books, over one shoulder and stuffed her coat through the other shoulder strap.

"That's a nice jacket," I said, looking at the soft, brown leather all crunched up inside the strap.

"Thanks. My dad bought it for me." Karianne frowned slightly.

"How come? I mean, for your birthday or something?"

"No. My sister just made the national team for skating. He bought her new skates and a plane ticket to England for the Commonwealth Games. The jacket was my consolation prize." Karianne walked off.

I stared after her. I wondered if Karianne even knew how lucky she was. My mom and dad — with three brothers eating us out of house and home — probably couldn't afford to buy me the sleeve of that jacket. Ashley could only dream of owning such a thing. But Karianne acted almost like she hated it.

Very strange.

* * *

"All right, girls," Mr. Jim said. "We have to stay focused on this game. We've got two losses now, due to unforeseen circumstances, but I think we're back on track. Ashley will be in goal, and that means our defence is up to full strength, since Karianne will be back in the line. I want to see everybody paying attention to shift changes — make sure you come off at my signal. We can't risk anyone getting tired out there. We need to stay strong. Let's go on some warm-up laps, then I want to see some passing drills."

The team broke out of its cluster. Most of us grabbed our water bottles for a last-minute drink. Emily yanked the elastic out of her hair and quickly re-did her ponytail. Karianne pulled off her hooded sweatshirt and unzipped her sports bag to toss it in.

I saw her stand still.

"What's the matter?" I asked, suddenly dreading the answer.

"My leather jacket's gone." Karianne's voice was low. "The one my dad gave me — you know."

I did know. My stomach sinking, I peered into her soccer bag. It was filled with extra soccer stuff, and a messy array of binders, notes and text books. No leather jacket. I found I had nothing to say.

"What's going on?" Mr. Jim asked.

"My leather jacket's missing," Karianne said calmly.

"Is there a chance you misplaced it?" Mr. Jim asked.

"No. It was in my soccer bag, and now it's gone. It's very expensive." She directed a look at Ashley, who was finishing her warm-up run. Breathing hard, she noticed all of us looking at her.

"What's going on?" she asked.

Mr. Jim was silent.

"Don't you think," Karianne said bitingly, "that it's a bit weird that lately nothing disappeared from the team — until *she* came back?"

Mr. Jim rubbed his chin thoughtfully.

"What's going on?" Ashley repeated, fear in her voice.

"Um … Karianne's jacket has disappeared. We were just going to start looking for it, weren't we?" I said.

Karianne turned on me viciously. "No, we weren't! There's no point in looking for it, because it's been stolen. Do you think Ashley stuffed it under a pine tree or something?"

Ashley's face had lost all colour.

Mr. Jim broke in. "There's no reason to accuse Ashley. We should have a look first, Karianne. Maybe it is around here somewhere."

"We don't have time to look!" Karianne lost all pretense of calm. "We have a game to play!"

Mr. Jim was immovable. "I'll ask the refs for a few minutes delay. Start searching, everybody."

The rest of the team had joined us by this point. Mr. Jim strode off to talk to the refs.

Karianne stood rock-firm and refused to search. "I want her gone," she said firmly, gesturing toward Ashley.

"*It wasn't me!*" Ashley yelled.

"Yeah, right!"

"Get over it, Karianne! I'm not the one who's ripping off stuff from the team, so leave it alone, okay?" Ashley's cheeks were red with anger and her hands were clenched into fists.

I stepped in between them. "Come on, help me look," I said to Ashley.

"For her stuff? Forget it." Ashley folded her arms and walked back on the field, where she watched from a distance.

The rest of the team was more helpful. Emily and Sarah began systematically lifting the jumble of jackets and soccer bags, looking inside the bags and backpacks. A few other girls checked in the nearby bushes and some of the parents who were waiting to watch the game helped, too.

Nobody seemed especially comfortable having their things searched. I opened my own bag and showed it to Sarah, so she could see it only held my sweatpants, soccer gear and water bottle. Karianne kept her overstuffed backpack close to her, as well as her soccer bag.

I held my breath as Emily opened Ashley's well-worn bag, then her knapsack. No jacket. I gave a sigh of relief. Ashley was off the hook from that angle, anyway. I glanced around, to see if there was anything we'd missed.

Karianne still had her arms folded, but there was something different about her. She looked like she was struggling to keep her face blank, yet I could see another emotion shining in her eyes. Was it — triumph?

I'd been assuming all along that someone had been taking the equipment because they needed or wanted it, but what if there was another reason?

Several facts collided in my mind. It was Sarah's stuff that had been stolen — until today. Aside from the money, the equipment had been stuff that either pulled Sarah from the game, or made her play really badly.

Who could have a motive for wanting Sarah out of the game? I narrowed my eyes at Karianne. Of course, Mr. Jim made Ashley the backup, but only *after* Sarah was pulled from the first game. Karianne had been furious. Then Teagan had gotten suspended. How easy it had been for suspicion to fall on Ashley — with a little help. Karianne had always been ready to point her finger at Ashley.

I frowned. Karianne's backpack looked awfully full, considering I had just seen her soccer bag full of homework and books.

Karianne caught me staring at her. My face must have given my thoughts away, because the trace of smugness I'd seen vanished and alarm took its place.

"Karianne, your bag is the only one that hasn't been searched," I announced.

"That's stupid," Emily said. "Why would Karianne's jacket be in her own bag, if it's been stolen?"

"Exactly." Karianne tightened her grip on the strap of her backpack and faced me defiantly. "Besides, you already saw inside my soccer bag."

"But not your backpack," I said softly. The whole team was looking at me.

Karianne knuckles turned white on the strap.

"How about you open it up?" I suggested, stepping forward.

"Jane, you're acting stupid," Karianne looked flustered. She stepped back.

I lunged. Karianne dodged, ripping the backpack out of my grasp, but not before I got a good grip on the canvas. There was a ripping sound as the zipper burst open, and folds of brown leather escaped from the opening.

A shocked murmur ran through the team.

Angry tears spurted up in Karianne's eyes.

"I hate you, Jane!" she spat. "And you, too, Ashley!" She glared at Ashley, grabbed her stuff and sprinted away from the field before anyone could stop her.

"Karianne had the jacket all along?" Emily looked confused. "But why? And what does she mean, she hates Ashley? What for?"

"It means," I answered slowly, "that Karianne's the one who's been stealing Sarah's stuff."

"I don't get it," Emily said.

"I think Karianne really wanted to play in goal this season. I'm not sure why it's so important to her, but she rigged it so that Sarah's equipment went missing. Then it was easy to blame Ashley, after everyone knew about her sister."

"But what about my birthday money?" Sarah demanded. "Did Karianne take that, too?"

"No." Ashley chewed on her lip. "Teagan did. I've been trying to find a way to give it back ever since, but everyone's been so suspicious — I did try once, but Jane caught me fiddling with your bag, and well … you know what she thought. I'm sorry, Sarah." Ashley opened her soccer bag, unzipped an inside pocket and handed Sarah an envelope.

Sarah took it wordlessly.

Mr. Jim hurried over. "Okay, they've agreed to let us start fifteen minutes late, because there's no other game booked on this field today —" He stopped. "*Where's Karianne?*"

"You'd better sit down, Mr. Jim," I said. "We have a lot to tell you."

15

Back on the Field

Mr. Jim's mouth tightened when we finished. He started to speak, but stopped when he saw the ref approaching. He held up one finger to indicate that he needed another minute, then turned back to us. "Okay, listen up. We only have a few seconds, and this is important."

"Karianne did a lot more here than embarrass herself in front of her team." Mr. Jim's expression was grim. "She took something from you, your trust. Sportsmanship, trust and communication are the keys to being a great team. The worst thing about all the suspicion and missing equipment in the last few weeks is that those qualities have disappeared."

Sarah snorted. "That depends on whose equipment got stolen," she muttered.

Mr. Jim ignored that. "You girls have the skill to be the best in the league, but if you don't have the team spirit to go with it, it's useless. Soccer isn't about one great player. It's about the team — it's for players who know that every person is important, not just one or two. I don't know why Karianne felt she had to steal Sarah's equipment to get herself into goal. But I'm guessing it didn't have anything to do with helping this team be the best it can be."

"That's for sure," Ashley said.

"I'll be speaking to Karianne and her parents, and temporarily suspending her from the team until this is sorted out,"

Mr. Jim continued.

"Coach, we need to start the game," the ref called.

"Okay!" Mr. Jim called over his shoulder, then grabbed his clipboard. "We're two players short today, with Sarah still off. Ashley, you take goal. Emily, I'm moving you up to play forward, and Jen, you move back to play sweeper. Mid-fielders and defence, I'll rotate you through to cover the positions for the switch, so don't expect to play your usual positions. Do your best, girls. If we lose today, we'll be so far down in the ranking, we won't make the playoffs."

I stripped off my sweatpants and joined the girls at the bench for a last-minute sip of water before running out onto the field.

"Win," Sarah said. The word was a fierce plea.

"You got it," I said. I turned to the rest of the team. "Don't let Karianne mess up this game for us. We have to forget about her and concentrate on soccer."

"Team cheer," Ashley said. We all put our fists into the centre. Everyone looked at each other soberly for a moment, then I took a deep breath. "Ready? One, two, three … *Goooooooooooo, Hurricanes!*" The shout burst from us, and I felt a sudden determination grip me. I was angry at Karianne, no question. But we had a game to play.

I jogged out to the center of the field and eyed my opponent. She was a big girl, much taller than me and heavier, mostly with muscle. I wondered briefly if I'd be able to outrun her. I'd have to rely on agility, I decided. Emily positioned herself on my right side, looking a little nervous. She didn't play forward very often, and not in such an important game, but Mr. Jim needed a more aggressive player like Jen back in sweeper. I gave her a quick smile and a thumbs-up before focusing on the other centre, who had twisted her torso in a last minute stretch. I glimpsed the number on the back of her jersey — Number 8.

The ref blew the whistle. I struck with my foot, fighting for the ball, but Number 8 overpowered me and thundered down the field. Once she left me behind, I had to struggle to catch up. I knew I wasn't doing a great job of covering her. Luckily, our defence did their job, and Jen snagged the ball before sending it to me with a wild kick. It bounced up high, and I jockeyed into position to try and head it toward the goal. "Emily!" I yelled.

I saw Emily move down the field, and I thumped the ball off my forehead toward her. I saw stars for a minute, then ran after the ball to help Emily, who was surrounded by opposing defence.

"Em, I'm open!" I called. Emily struggled to get a clear shot, but she was blocked every time she turned around. Number 8 was now beside me, doing everything possible to prevent me from getting an opening.

Their defence wrestled the ball away and sent it back down the field. Number 8 sprinted after it, leaving me in her dust. She was such a powerhouse that our defence seemed to crumble at her onslaught, and no one could get the ball away from her. One of their forwards was ready at the side of the goal…Number 8 sent a crisp pass to her and the forward fired it toward our goal. Ashley thrust her hands reflexively to the side and the ball glanced off. Number 8 was right there for the rebound and dealt the ball a mighty kick. Ashley leaped.

"Ooof!" I heard her grunt, smothering the ball into her midriff. She landed unsteadily, then kicked the ball out. Our players on the bench cheered, Sarah in particular. "Way to go, Ashley!" she hollered.

"You okay?" Jen asked Ashley, who was clutching her stomach.

"Yeah," I heard Ashley gasp. I was too busy sprinting down the field to catch up with the ball. Mr. Jim signalled for Emily and I to come off. One of our girls who usually played mid-field was already on as left forward, and two more were ready to play.

"Rest," said Mr. Jim when we reached the bench. "You'll need it. This is going to be a tough game."

I was breathing so hard, I didn't bother to answer. I took

small sips of water and watched the action unfolding on the field. Both teams seemed fairly equal in skill, which was good, but we had fewer players, so we weren't able to switch as often. Both teams fought for the ball, and the players seemed to be doing a lot of running up and down the field.

"Pass, girls! Look for an opening!" Mr. Jim yelled.

By halftime, I was shaking with fatigue and sweat was rolling off me. My jersey felt uncomfortably damp. "Try to pass more, Jane," Mr. Jim advised. "Pass whenever you can. Save your energy."

I nodded and slurped gratefully on one of the popsicles that someone's parents had provided for the team. When the game resumed, I tried not to run so much, and to pass more, but Number 8 kept me covered. My only hope was to dodge her, and that took energy. Both teams were getting tired, struggling to keep possession. Ashley deflected another shot on our goal, but we couldn't seem to get the ball back down the field. The minutes wore down, and neither team had scored.

When I switched off near the end of the second half, Mr. Jim checked his watch. "Your next shift will probably be the last. Stay out there until the whistle, unless I signal you off, okay?"

"Okay."

The seconds ticked past. Mr. Jim glanced at his watch. "Okay, Jane, Emily. Time." He signalled the forwards off. Kara, who was usually one of our mid-fielders, Emily and I jogged to the forwards' positions on the field.

Number 8 was back in the line, too. She gave me a wolfish grin, but I stood as tall as I could and didn't back away, fighting instead to get clear. Jen had just gotten possession down by our goal.

Our mid-fielders passed it up. I heard someone holler, "Jane!" I dodged around Number 8 just in time to snag the ball. I ran hard, dribbling toward their goal. I could hear Number 8 pounding behind me. Emily was barricaded behind the defence

— I had no one to pass to. I flashed back to the tryouts, when I collided with Karianne. I had failed then — but I wouldn't fail now. I searched frantically for someone to pass to, but no one was clear. I couldn't even pass back, because Number 8 was right behind me, breathing fire down my neck.

"Jane! *Take the shot!*" I heard Mr. Jim bellow.

I was still a long way from the goal, but I reared my foot back in mid-stride and aimed for the upper corner of the goal. The ball flew like a bullet, whistling as it whirled, the black and white markings blurring in the air. The goalie dived, arms outstretched, but fell short as the ball buried itself into the net.

"Yes!" I punched my fist into the air. I could see the ref counting down the seconds, and heard the three sharp blasts from the whistle. The game was over, 1–0, Hurricanes. We'd won!

16

Teacher Trouble

I was exhausted. I lay collapsed on my bed, my head hanging off the side. My bones hurt, my feet ached, one thigh muscle kept going into spasm, which was driving me nuts, and I had a headache. Even my toenails were sore. But winning that game meant we were still in the playoffs, and we did it in spite of all that garbage with Karianne. I couldn't stop my face from breaking into a smile.

"Oh, by the way, Jane," Mom stopped in my doorway and held out an envelope. "This came in the mail for you today."

"Thanks. Can you just leave it on my desk?" I didn't think I could move.

Mom put the envelope onto a pile of homework. "You played a great game today."

"We really needed to win this one."

Mom was silent. She knew some of what had happened with Karianne, but not all. No one really knew all of it, except Karianne. "Well, I think you deserved it," Mom said. She leaned over and pressed a kiss on my forehead.

I smiled as she left, my eye catching the white of the envelope. I don't usually get much mail. I used to have a pen pal, but we stopped writing months ago. I wondered if it could be from the magazine contest, but it was kind of soon. Ashley and I had only mailed in the recipe a week ago.

I slid off the bed and picked up the envelope. My name was typed on the front, and the return address was from *TeenWorld* magazine. Probably just a thank-you for entering the contest or something, I thought. But my heart hammered against my chest as I slit the envelope open with my thumb.

I unfolded the letter.

Dear Jane Evans,
Congratulations! We are pleased to announce that you are the winner of the TeenWorld *CookFest competition, with your entry recipe for Strawberry Muffins. The judges agreed that this simple recipe achieved excellent results ....*

I skipped the next part, my eyes scanning to the end.

You will be contacted by phone to arrange for a photo session and interview to run in the magazine, and to arrange for receipt of your prizes.
Thank you again for entering the TeenWorld *CookFest.*

Sincerely,
Angela Crawford
Publisher

I let out a screech of joy. "Mom! Mom! Dad! Adam, Trent, Joey! Come here! *Right now!*"

There was a thundering of feet.

"What!"

"What?"

"What's going on? Are you all right?" Dad elbowed his way through the boys.

"I won! I really won!" My smile came right from inside my heart. "Can you believe it?"

"Won what?" Mom asked.

"The CookFest." I handed her the letter. "Remember, the boys told you about it?"

"I knew you would, Janey," Adam said.

"Those muffins are the best," Trent agreed.

"That's terrific, honey." Dad had been reading over Mom's shoulder and reached down to give me a hug.

Mom grinned. "You won an education bond, plus a shopping spree? That's what I call a prize!" She hugged me, too. "You'll have to make those muffins for us sometime."

"I already did. The boys ate them all," I answered. I moved toward the door. "I have to phone Ashley!"

* * *

I knocked softly on Ms. Horvath's classroom door. Ashley gave me an encouraging thumbs-up from further down the hall.

"Come in."

I pushed open the door.

"Jane." Ms. Horvath looked up from her desk, where she was grading papers with a red pen. "What can I do for you." She didn't make it sound like a question.

I took a fresh grip on my courage. "I wanted to talk to you about my grade in Foods."

Ms. Horvath eyed me. "Jane, I'm a little busy right now."

"I'm sorry, but this will only take a minute," I said firmly. "I tried to speak to you the day the fundraising money went missing, and you didn't have time for me then, either."

Ms. Horvath sighed through her nose and laid down her pen. "All right. What do you want to say?"

"I wanted to tell you that I don't think I deserve to fail your class. I really can cook."

"I haven't seen any evidence of that," Ms. Horvath said.

I brandished the CookFest letter. "Maybe this will help."

Ms. Horvath read it, eyebrows lifted. "This is wonderful, Jane, but it doesn't change your grade."

"How can you say that? Winning this contest proves that I can cook at least as well as anybody in my class, probably better."

"Jane, my class involves more that being able to cook something edible. It involves following directions, working within a group, and achieving adequate exam and assignment scores. So far, you've shown me that you aren't capable of any of those things."

"That's not fair! I am! I tried hard in your class, even though I made some mistakes, and I offered to do make-up assignments, but you wouldn't let me. I won a national cooking contest, and you won't consider passing me?"

"One has nothing to do with the other. For all I know, you've never made strawberry muffins in your life, and this recipe belonged to your grandmother. I can't change a grade based on something I haven't seen you do."

My lips tightened into a grim line. "So basically, you're saying I cheated."

Ms. Horvath contemplated me. "No, I'm not saying that."

"Yes, I think you are." I marched from the room.

"Jane, wait!" I heard Ms. Horvath call after me, but I stomped down the hall, so furious I felt as thought I was foaming at the mouth. Ashley had to run to catch up.

"What happened?" she asked.

"She told me I cheated."

"What!"

I explained everything, still going full blast down the hall.

"What are you going to do now?" Ashley asked.

"The only thing left to do," I said. "Talk to the principal." We had reached the office door. I burst in, confronting the startled secretary. "I need to speak to Mr. Wentworth. Right away, please."

"I believe he's in a meeting. Shouldn't you be going to class?"

"I need to see Mr. Wentworth first."

The secretary gave me a measuring glance. She must have judged by my face that I had something serious to discuss, because she stood up. "I'll see how long he's going to be."

She returned within a few seconds. "He says you may go in."

"Hello there, Jane. What's on your mind?" He gestured for me to sit.

I took the nearest chair and sat on the edge, momentarily tongue-tied. It was a relief that Mr. Wentworth remembered who I was — probably from when I played on the school basketball team — but now that I didn't need to introduce myself, I wasn't quite sure where to begin.

"I have a complaint," I said at last.

"I see." Mr. Wentworth leaned back in his chair. "Problems with another student?"

"No, sir. With one of the teachers."

Mr. Wentworth brought his chair forward with a clunk. "A teacher? In what way, exactly?"

"Well …." I paused, choosing my words carefully. "I believe that I've received an unfair grade. A failing grade."

"Shouldn't you be discussing this with the teacher?" Mr. Wentworth seemed suddenly impatient.

"I already have. She was not … reasonable."

This earned an uplifted eyebrow. "Really? Well, perhaps you should tell me the story, then."

And so, I did. I tried to be as fair as possible about my mistakes in class, and how I deserved low marks on those assignments. But I also mentioned asking to do make-up assignments and being told no, and then I showed him the contest letter.

Mr. Wentworth looked very pleased when he read it. "Jane, this really fantastic. This a national magazine contest you've won."

"I know. And I won it with a recipe that was all my own. I didn't deserve to have Ms. Horvath suggest I cheated in the contest." Then I explained about Ms. Horvath's comments.

Mr. Wentworth tapped his pen against his chin, then tossed it on the desk and stood up. "It seems to me," he said, "that there's only one thing left to do."

"What's that?" I asked.

"Make Ms. Horvath some strawberry muffins."

17

Recipe for Success

"Mr. Wentworth, I really don't think this is necessary." Ms. Horvath set her lips in a prim line.

"Jane has asked to do extra assignments to make her grade. I think that if she does a good job on this one, we should consider raising her mark above failing."

"But Mr. Wentworth, Jane has had ample opportunity in class to improve her marks, and she has not shown any effort there at all."

Mr. Wentworth didn't yield. "I understand that you believe that, but I think Jane deserves a chance. She has taken the time to speak to both of us about the problem, so she obviously cares about her mark in this class."

Ms. Horvath looked extremely annoyed. "I have a lot of papers to mark. I don't have time to supervise her right now."

"That's fine. I'll watch out for her."

Ms. Horvath repressed a snort. "Easier said than done."

The anger inside me was growing. I'd gone from not really liking Ms. Horvath's class to despising it. Why wouldn't she at least give me a chance?

"All right, Jane." Mr. Wentworth took off his suit jacket, reached for an apron and tied it around his waist. "Let's get to work."

I bit the inside of my cheek to stop from grinning. Mr. Wentworth looked pretty funny in a flowered apron. He'd chosen Ms.

Horvath's. I pulled on a plain white one and led the way to a kitchen station.

"First," I said. "We have to make sure we have all the ingredients."

"Check," said Mr. Wentworth.

I dug through the cupboards and the refrigerator until I had everything we needed on the counter. "Now we need a big mixing bowl, the blender and two wooden spoons."

"Check," said Mr. Wentworth. He watched as I assembled those items next to the ingredients. "Now what?"

"Now we make muffins," I answered. I showed him step-by-step how I measured and mixed the strawberry muffins. When they were finally in the oven and the timer was set, I noticed Ms. Horvath, who had been marking papers at her desk the whole time, had been listening, and slowly her face lost its hostile expression.

She got up and came over. "Jane, I heard all of that. Why on earth didn't you work like that in my class?"

I shifted. "I don't know."

Ms. Horvath and Mr. Wentworth waited.

"Because it's boring, I guess. I like to make up things as I go along, and I don't always follow every recipe exactly, the way you make us do in class. You got mad when I put all that flour in the cookie dough, but I *was* following the recipe. It was the recipe that was wrong. And sometimes I'd make mistakes, like with separating the eggs, but that's because I never bother with those kinds of tools at home. I just *do* it, you know?"

"But Jane, that's my job. I have to teach students the rules, so they learn to cook," Ms. Horvath objected.

"But sometimes when you don't follow the rules in cooking, you get some amazing results," I said.

Ms. Horvath looked thoughtful. "All this time I've been assuming that you weren't interested in cooking and were goofing off in class, when maybe you're too good a cook for food basics. I didn't realize you were bored. I thought you just weren't interested in trying."

The timer rang, and the warm smell of fresh muffins filled the air.

"I'd say those were done," said Mr. Wentworth. "How about we give them a try?"

I pulled on some oven mitts and took the tray out of the oven. The muffins were still piping hot when I put three on a plate, and I waited while Ms. Horvath and Mr. Wentworth took a bite.

"Well?" I said. I couldn't stand the suspense any longer.

Ms. Horvath and Mr. Wentworth looked at each other and smiled.

"I'd say you passed," Ms. Horvath answered.

18

Decisions

W hat a relief!" I said to Ashley at lunchtime. I'd already told her the whole story. We were coming back to school from the convenience store, sharing a small bag of potato chips to celebrate as we walked.

"No kidding. That took major guts, to go to Wentworth like that."

"No — desperation," I said, grinning. "I just didn't want to have to quit soccer."

We reached the crosswalk by the school, and I pounded on the button for the walk signal. Ashley reached for the potato-chip bag, glanced up, then froze. I followed her gaze.

Karianne was walking toward us. Her head was down — she hadn't seen us yet. Ashley stood very still.

When Karianne looked up, her expression went blank. It was hard to tell what she was thinking. Ashley's face was easier to read. Jaw clenched, mouth drawn into a grim line, I could see the anger darken her eyes. I held my breath.

Karianne stopped before she reached us, but Ashley stepped forward. And waited.

"What?" Karianne said at last.

"An 'I'm sorry' might be nice," Ashley said.

Karianne blinked.

"You made everybody believe I was a thief! Everyone believed your stupid rumors — at school, at soccer. How could you do that? How could you lie like that?"

"Your sister created more rumours than I ever did," Karianne retorted. "So don't put all the blame on me."

Ashley was speechless with rage. She flung her hand up, but I caught it before she could crack Karianne across the face, which was what I was sure she was about to do.

Ashley wrestled free. "I'm *not* going to hit her!" she snapped. "Even though I want to." She turned back to Karianne, who looked scared. "Teagan was a loser for stealing. No question. But she never hurt anybody like you tried to hurt me. You're a horrible, mean person. Everybody on the team hates you, and they're glad you're gone. Because not only are you a liar, you can't even play. You're the worst player on the team!" Ashley stopped. She was breathing hard, her fists clenched.

I winced. That was pretty vicious. Karianne's face had gone white. She was shaking, and for once, she couldn't keep her expression neutral. Her face crumpled — she was crying.

"I'm sorry, okay?" Karianne sobbed. "I'm really, really sorry! I didn't mean for it to happen like that — it just did. I took Sarah's cleats because I thought if she couldn't play in goal, Mr. Jim might put me in. And then he made you backup goalie, and…well, I just needed to be in goal, that's all, and I was scared of getting caught. It was easy to blame you, and I didn't think about how you felt. I'm sorry, Ashley. I mean it."

But Ashley, for once, was immovable. "Why did you do it?" she demanded.

"I wanted to be goalie. It's the most important position on the field, and it's the only position I'm halfway good at. I thought maybe if you quit the team, I'd get a chance to play."

"Karianne, every position is important," I said. "Soccer is a team sport. Everyone works together."

"Yeah, but the goalie gets the glory. The goalie and the striker, and I'm not good enough to be striker," she said.

"But —" I stopped. I wasn't sure what to say.

Ashley narrowed her eyes. "You still haven't told us why being goalie was so important — important enough to steal."

Karianne looked down. "Do you have any idea how embarrassing it is to be the sister of a famous athlete and have everyone wonder why you suck at sports?"

We were silent.

"Everyone expects me to be a good athlete, but I'm not. I'm not that good at soccer. I know that. I'm not even that good in goal, and that's my best position." Karianne took a deep breath. "I'll never be like my sister, no matter how hard I try. Karianne's eyes filled with tears. "I never will be. And I hate it."

I swallowed hard. "Karianne, it's all right." I touched her shoulder.

Karianne snuffled and wiped her nose on the sleeve of her jacket. "How would you know, Jane — Miss Super-Jock of the Century?"

"So? I still know what it feels like when someone expects you to be something you're not."

"Like when?" Karianne demanded.

"Like in Ms. Horvath's class. She always expects me to mess up."

Karianne frowned. "School doesn't count."

"Yeah it does. Feeling stupid isn't limited to sports." I answered.

"I guess," Karianne said. "But now I've blown it with the team. Like Ashley said, everyone hates me — and I guess I can't blame them. I was pretty dumb, taking all that stuff. I don't know why I ever thought it would work."

Ashley chewed on her lip. "You know, Karianne, I want to hate you. I really do."

Karianne stared at her fingers. "I know."

"But," Ashley continued. "I know how you feel about your sister … sort of, anyway."

Karianne looked up. "You do?"

"I spend half my life trying to make people believe I'm not like Teagan. Just like Jane said, people assume that I'm like her, without even taking time to know me. I hate it, too."

"But people can see just by looking at you that you're not like Teagan," I said. "You're not into green hair and fake tattoos and weird clothes."

"Yeah, but that doesn't matter. I know I don't look like Teagan, but people sometimes judge the kind of person you are because of your family or your background or how much money your parents make." Ashley turned to Karianne. "I know it's different for you. Deirdre is like the opposite — she's the best, and Teagan's the worst, but you and I don't have to be what other people expect us to be."

"Teagan's not so bad," I muttered, thinking of what she told me about their family's divorce. "She just deals with problems differently."

Ashley looked at me like I was crazy.

Karianne took a deep breath. "Do you think the team might let me come back?"

"Would you really want to?" I asked.

"I really like soccer. Even if I'm not that good, I still like it."

I glanced at Ashley. "I think if you explained everything to the team and Mr. Jim, they might let you come back. But probably it's Ashley who you should be asking."

Karianne bit her lip and said nothing.

The bell sounded from the school.

"Come on, we're going to be late," Ashley said.

Karianne didn't move. "What about the team?"

"Karianne," Ashley stopped, a pained expression on her face. "Look, I get it now. I know it's tough, trying to be as good as your sister. But …." Ashley paused and looked her straight in the eye. "I still don't think you should come back." Then she turned and headed toward the school.

19

Team Spirit

Saturday morning dawned bright and sunny, and the whole team showed up early for the game. Mr. Jim had asked us to be there in time for a team meeting and a short practice session before we had to play.

This was the kind of soccer morning that I lived for. It just felt so good to be out there, in the fresh wind and warm sunshine, running warm-up laps around the field. Ashley jogged silently beside me and we passed a ball back and forth as we ran. I just let myself go and enjoyed the feeling of my legs pounding on the grass and the breeze blowing through my hair. It felt like forever since I stopped worrying about other things and just had fun playing soccer.

Mr. Jim blew his whistle, and we gathered near the bench.

"Girls," he began. "I wanted you all to come early today so we could talk about our team situation."

"You mean, for the playoffs?" Sarah asked.

"Well, indirectly, I guess. How well we do in the playoffs will depend a lot on how our team is functioning in the next few weeks. What I really mean is how we are going to deal with our situation with Karianne." He held up his hand to ward off comments. "Now, technically, I have no idea if she can be removed from the team for the rest of the season. Her parents have paid her registration, and I suspect some sort of formal complaint would have to be filed with the soccer association. I gave her a three-game suspension and spoke to her parents, but she will be returning after this game unless I take further action. I want to ask you kids how you feel about her rejoining the team after what she did."

Sarah spoke out. "I don't want her back. Nobody can trust her after this."

"Me neither," said Emily.

"Well, keep in mind that we would be entering the playoffs short on defense. That means we need a lot more switching off to keep the field covered. We don't have enough players for a full shift change as it is," Mr. Jim said. "There's no question that we can use Karianne. She's been good in defence."

Sarah snorted. "Yeah, right. In what way, exactly?"

"Give her a break," I snapped, surprising myself. "She played goalie last year, Sarah. So she messed up in defence a few times. She's learning the position."

"Jane's right," Mr. Jim said. "Karianne might not be as technically skilled as some of you, but she helped to keep our defence solid, and that's what we need heading into the playoffs."

"Yeah, but what about all that stuff you told us about team spirit?" Sarah said. "If we can't trust her, we can't be a team. And let's face it, the girl's a thief."

"No, she's not," I said abruptly. "She's not like that."

"What are you talking about?" Sarah demanded. "Of course she is! She ripped off half my soccer stuff."

"I know, but she did it because she wanted to play in goal, not because she wanted your stuff," I said.

"Oh, so sabotage is, like, a good reason for stealing?" Sarah said sarcastically.

"No!" I felt frustrated. Ashley and I exchanged glances. We were the only ones who knew why Karianne wanted to do well in sports. "But she had some reasons for what she did."

"Oh, well, someday if you feel like explaining it to us, let us know, okay?" Sarah huffed.

The rest of the team nodded in agreement. "Yeah," they muttered.

I felt helpless. I could understand why they were angry. They had every right to be, especially Sarah. The problem was, part of me was still mad at Karianne, and the other part was remembering how sad she looked when she said she would never be as good as her sister. I stole another glance at Ashley, and I could tell she was remembering, too.

"Maybe she's sorry," Ashley said suddenly.

The team fell silent. I turned to look at Ashley. "I thought you didn't want her back," I said.

Ashley shrugged. "Maybe. But if she came back, I bet she wouldn't do it again. Why would she? She knows she'll get blamed right away."

"But why did she do it?" Emily asked.

"Her sister is probably going to the next Olympics," I said. "She's awesome and Karianne felt like she had to be just as good."

"That's so lame, to be that desperate," Sarah said in disgust.

"Yeah? Well, wait until you get punted out of goal because Ashley's better than you, and see how you feel," I snapped, my temper rising.

Mr. Jim stepped in. "This isn't helping us decide whether to allow Karianne back on the team."

The ref walked over to us. "Coach, you ready to play?"

Mr. Jim nodded. "Give us one second." He turned back to us. "Well? Decision time. Yes or no?"

Ashley and I looked at each other.

"Yes," Ashley said. "Let her come back."

"Yeah," I said, and most of the team nodded.

Mr. Jim clapped his hands. "Okay, ladies. Let's go! We've got a game to play."

Sarah looked sour. "If one more thing goes missing …." She let the thought drift off as she pulled on her goalie gloves on and trotted out onto the field.

Ashley and I were taking the second shift. We moved down toward the end of the bench. I was just about to ask Ashley why she changed her mind, when someone spoke.

"Thanks, Ashley," Karianne said softly. She was standing behind us, her hands full of Sarah's equipment.

We swivelled in shock. "Karianne! What are you doing here?" I exclaimed.

She held up the equipment. "I wanted to bring this back to Sarah." She hesitated. "I heard what you guys said. I was standing just behind the bench." Karianne managed a smile. "Thanks, both of you. I really mean it. They would've tossed me out without you."

I thought of how it must have felt, to hear Sarah trashing her, and have the rest of the team debating about whether to let her come back. I thought about what we had talked about, about how unfair it is when people judge others without knowing the whole story, without even considering second chances. I glanced at Ashley, and could tell she was thinking about Teagan, the same way I was thinking about Ms. Horvath.

I gave a half-shrug and smiled. "Welcome back."

Jane's Strawberry Muffins

Yum!

In a big bowl, dump in:
2 big handfuls of flour (2 cups)
1 small handful of sugar (2/3 cup)
1 big sprinkle of baking powder (2 1/2 tsp)
1 very small sprinkle of baking soda (1/4 tsp)
2 good shakes from the salt shaker (1/2 tsp)
Stir a couple of times with a wooden spoon.

In the blender, dump in:
12 frozen strawberries (about 1 1/2 cups)
1 splot of sour cream (1/3 cup)
A chunk of butter, melted in the microwave (1/2 cup)
Some milk (1/4 cup)
1 egg

Turn blender on and mix until everything turns pink and smooth. Add this glop to the stuff in the bowl and stir a few times with the wooden spoon. Turn oven on to 375º. Spray muffin tins with non-stick spray and fill halfway with dough. Bake for about 25 minutes, until tops are lightly browned and a toothpick comes out clean.

Mmm! Don't they smell terrific?!!

Other books you'll enjoy in the Sports Stories series

Baseball

❏ *Curve Ball* by John Danakas #1
Tom Poulos is looking forward to a summer of baseball in Toronto until his mother puts him on a plane to Winnipeg.

❏ *Baseball Crazy* by Martyn Godfrey #10
Rob Carter wins an all-expenses-paid chance to be bat boy at the Blue Jays spring training camp in Florida.

❏ *Shark Attack* by Judi Peers #25
The East City Sharks have a good chance of winning the county championship until their arch rivals get a tough new pitcher.

❏ *Hit and Run* by Dawn Hunter and Karen Hunter #35
Glen Thomson is a talented pitcher, but as his ego inflates, team morale plummets. Will he learn from being benched for losing his temper?

❏ *Power Hitter* by C. A. Forsyth #41
Connor's summer was looking like a write-off. That is, until he discovered his secret talent.

❏ *Sayonara, Sharks* by Judi Peers #48
In this sequel to *Shark Attack*, Ben and Kate are excited about the school trip to Japan, but Matt's not sure he wants to go.

Basketball

❏ *Fast Break* by Michael Coldwell #8
Moving from Toronto to small-town Nova Scotia was rough, but when Jeff makes the school basketball team he thinks things are looking up.

❏ *Camp All-Star* by Michael Coldwell #12
In this insider's view of a basketball camp, Jeff Lang encounters some unexpected challenges.

❏ *Nothing but Net* by Michael Coldwell #18
The Cape Breton Grizzly Bears prepare for an out-of-town basketball tournament they're sure to lose.

❏ *Slam Dunk* by Steven Barwin and Gabriel David Tick #23
In this sequel to *Roller Hockey Blues*, Mason Ashbury's basketball team adjusts to the arrival of some new players: girls.

❏ *Courage on the Line* by Cynthia Bates #33
After Amelie changes schools, she must confront difficult former teammates in an extramural match.

❏ *Free Throw* by Jacqueline Guest #34
Matthew Eagletail must adjust to a new school, a new team and a new father along with five pesky sisters.

❏ *Triple Threat* by Jacqueline Guest #38
Matthew's cyber-pal Free Throw comes to visit, and together they face a bully on the court.

❏ *Queen of the Court* by Michele Martin Bossley #40
What happens when the school's fashion queen winds up on the basketball court?

❏ *Shooting Star* by Cynthia Bates #46
Quyen is dealing with a troublesome teammate on her new basketball team, as well as trouble at home. Her parents seem haunted by something that happened in Vietnam.

❏ *Home Court Advantage* by Sandra Diersch #51
Debbie had given up hope of being adopted, until the Lowells came along. Things were looking up, until Debbie is accused of stealing from the team.

❏ *Rebound* by Adrienne Mercer #54
C.J.'s dream in life is to play on the national basketball team. But one day she wakes up in pain and can barely move her joints, much less be a star player.

Figure Skating
❏ *A Stroke of Luck* by Kathryn Ellis #6
Strange accidents are stalking one of the skaters at the Millwood Arena.

❏ *The Winning Edge* by Michele Martin Bossley #28
Jennie wants more than anything to win a gruelling series of competitions, but is success worth losing her friends?

❏ *Leap of Faith* by Michele Martin Bossley #36
Amy wants to win at any cost, until an injury makes skating almost impossible. Will she go on?

Gymnastics

❏ *The Perfect Gymnast* by Michele Martin Bossley #9
Abby's new friend has all the confidence she needs, but she also has a serious problem that nobody but Abby seems to know about.

Ice Hockey

❏ *Two Minutes for Roughing* by Joseph Romain #2
As a new player on a tough Toronto hockey team, Les must fight to fit in.

❏ *Hockey Night in Transcona* by John Danakas #7
Cody Powell gets promoted to the Transcona Sharks' first line, bumping out the coach's son, who's not happy with the change.

❏ *Face Off* by C. A. Forsyth #13
A talented hockey player finds himself competing with his best friend for a spot on a select team.

❏ *Hat Trick* by Jacqueline Guest #20
The only girl on an all-boy hockey team works to earn the captain's respect and her mother's approval.

❏ *Hockey Heroes* by John Danakas #22
A left-winger on the thirteen-year-old Transcona Sharks adjusts to a new best friend and his mom's boyfriend.

❏ *Hockey Heat Wave* by C. A. Forsyth #27
In this sequel to *Face Off*, Zack and Mitch run into trouble when it looks as if only one of them will make the select team at hockey camp.

❏ *Shoot to Score* by Sandra Richmond #31
Playing defense on the B list alongside the coach's mean-spirited son is a tough obstacle for Steven to overcome, but he perseveres and changes his luck.

❏ *Rookie Season* by Jacqueline Guest #42
What happens when a boy wants to join an all-girl hockey team?

❏ *Brothers on Ice* by John Danakas #44
Brothers Dylan and Deke both want to play goal for the same team.

❏ *Rink Rivals* by Jacqueline Guest #49
A move to Calgary finds the Evans twins pitted against each other on the ice, and struggling to help each other out of trouble.

❏ *Power Play* by Michele Martin Bossley #50
An early-season injury causes Zach Thomas to play timidly, and a school bully just makes matters worse. Will a famous hockey player will be able to help Zach sort things out?

Riding

❏ *A Way with Horses* by Peter McPhee #11
A young Alberta rider, invited to study show jumping at a posh local riding school, uncovers a secret.

❏ *Riding Scared* by Marion Crook #15
A reluctant new rider struggles to overcome her fear of horses.

❏ *Katie's Midnight Ride* by C. A. Forsyth #16
An ambitious barrel racer finds herself without a horse weeks before her biggest rodeo.

❏ *Glory Ride* by Tamara L. Williams #21
Chloe Anderson fights memories of a tragic fall for a place on the Ontario Young Riders Team.

❏ *Cutting It Close* by Marion Crook #24
In this novel about barrel racing, a young rider finds her horse is in trouble just as she's about to compete in an important event.

❏ *Shadow Ride* by Tamara L. Williams #37
Bronwen has to choose between competing aggressively for herself or helping out a teammate.

Roller Hockey

❏ *Roller Hockey Blues* by Steven Barwin and Gabriel David Tick #17
Mason Ashbury faces a summer of boredom until he makes the roller hockey team.

Running
❏ *Fast Finish* by Bill Swan #30
Noah is a promising young runner headed for the provincial finals when he suddenly decides to withdraw from the event.

Sailing
❏ *Sink or Swim* by William Pasnak #5
Dario can barely manage the dog paddle, but thanks to his mother he's spending the summer at a water sports camp.

Soccer
❏ *Lizzie's Soccer Showdown* by John Danakas #3
When Lizzie asks why the boys and girls can't play together, she finds herself the new captain of the soccer team.

❏ *Alecia's Challenge* by Sandra Diersch #32
Thirteen-year-old Alecia has to cope with a new school, a new step-father, and friends who have suddenly discovered the opposite sex.

❏ *Shut-Out!* by Camilla Reghelini Rivers #39
David wants to play soccer more than anything, but will the new coach let him?

❏ *Offside!* by Sandra Diersch #43
Alecia has to confront a new girl who drives her teammates crazy.

❏ *Heads Up!* by Dawn Hunter and Karen Hunter #45
Do the Warriors really need a new, hot-shot player who skips practice?

❏ *Off the Wall* by Camilla Reghelini Rivers #52
Lizzie loves indoor soccer, and she's thrilled when her little sister gets into the sport. But when their teams are pitted against each other, Lizzie can only warn her sister to watch out.

❏ *Trapped!* by Michele Martin Bossley #53
There's a thief on Jane's soccer team, and everyone thinks it's her best friend, Ashley. Jane must find the true culprit to save both Ashley and the team's morale.

Swimming

❏ *Breathing Not Required* by Michele Martin Bossley #4
Gracie works so hard to be chosen for the solo at synchronized swimming that she almost loses her best friend in the process.

❏ *Water Fight!* by Michele Martin Bossley #14
Josie's perfect sister is driving her crazy, but when she takes up swimming — Josie's sport — it's too much to take.

❏ *Taking a Dive* by Michele Martin Bossley #19
Josie holds the provincial record for the butterfly, but in this sequel to Water Fight! she can't seem to match her own time and might not go on to the nationals.

❏ *Great Lengths* by Sandra Diersch #26
Fourteen-year-old Jessie decides to find out whether the rumours about a new swimmer at her Vancouver club are true.

❏ *Pool Princess* by Michele Martin Bossley #47
In this sequel to *Breathing Not Required*, Gracie must deal with a bully on the new synchro team in Calgary.

Track and Field

❏ *Mikayla's Victory* by Cynthia Bates #29
Mikayla must compete against her friend if she wants to represent her school at an important track event.

❏ *Walker's Runners* by Robert Rayner #55
Toby Morton hates gym. In fact, he doesn't run for anything — except the classroom door. Then Mr. Walker arrives and persuades Toby to join the running team.